Sarah,

Oh, My Dragon

I Like Big Dragons Series - Book 3

LANI LYNN VALE

Lani Lynn Vale

Copyright © 2016 Lani Lynn Vale

All rights reserved.

**ISBN-13:
978-1545144961**

**ISBN-10:
1545144966**

Dedication

This one is dedicated to my mom. If you hadn't urged me to follow my dreams, I wouldn't have the life that I do right now, doing what I love. Thank you. I love you.

Acknowledgements

Marisa-Rose Shor, you made this cover freakin' beautiful, thank you so much.

Kellie Montgomery—You're an amazing editor, and thank you so much for getting to this so fast and never yelling at me for the short notice!

Danielle Palumbo—I couldn't do this without you. You're amazing! The amount of time and effort you put into making these beauties shine is amazing, and I'm truly blessed to have found you.

CONTENTS

Chapter 1- Page 9
Chapter 2- Page 23
Chapter 3- Page 37
Chapter 4- Page 51
Chapter 5- Page 67
Chapter 6- Page 75
Chapter 7- Page 79
Chapter 8- Page 89
Chapter 9- Page 101
Chapter 10- Page 113
Chapter 11- Page 121
Chapter 12- Page 133
Chapter 13- Page 145
Chapter 14- Page 149
Chapter 15- Page 157
Chapter 16- Page 165
Chapter 17- Page 175
Chapter 18- Page 183
Chapter 19- Page 189
Chapter 20- Page 195
Chapter 21- Page 201
Chapter 22- Page 211
Chapter 23- Page 225
Chapter 24- Page 231
Chapter 25- Page 243
Chapter 26- Page 249

Other Titles by Lani Lynn Vale:
The Freebirds

Boomtown

Highway Don't Care

Another One Bites the Dust

Last Day of My Life

Texas Tornado

I Don't Dance

The Heroes of The Dixie Wardens MC

Lights To My Siren

Halligan To My Axe

Kevlar To My Vest

Keys To My Cuffs

Life To My Flight

Charge To My Line

Counter To My Intelligence

Right To My Wrong

Code 11- KPD SWAT

Center Mass

Double Tap

Oh, My Dragon

Bang Switch

Execution Style

Charlie Foxtrot

Kill Shot

Coup De Grace

The Uncertain Saints

Whiskey Neat

Jack & Coke

Vodka On The Rocks

Bad Apple

Dirty Mother

Rusty Nail

The Kilgore Fire Series

Shock Advised

Flash Point

Oxygen Deprived

Controlled Burn

Put Out

I Like Big Dragons Series

I Like Big Dragons and I Cannot Lie

Dragons Need Love, Too

Oh, My Dragon

The Dixie Warden Rejects

Beard Mode

Fear the Beard (3-30-17)

Son of a Beard (4-27-17)

CHAPTER 1

Some girls watched Beauty and the Beast and wanted the prince. I want the library.
-Meme

Wink

The stairs screamed in protest as I made my way back down the ladder.

I hated my job.

Well and truly hated it; I had no clue why I continued to do it when I hated it so much.

In fact, if I'd just quit already, I would be free to do my photography full time.

But that was the thing about me. I hated quitting. *Anything.*

It didn't matter what it was.

A sport. A novel. A job.

They were all the same in my book.

Not to mention that I had no guarantee that next month would be as good as this month.

Christmas was now over, and I'd realized that if I managed to get at least six clients a month, I could make enough to carry me through until next month.

I also sold my photography as well. Anything I was able to sell was an added bonus that gave me a tiny cushion and made everything a little bit easier.

But my brain was still stuck in 'poor' mode. Meaning that I couldn't quit. Not when my mind still had me eating Ramen noodles when my bank account clearly could accommodate Velveeta mac and cheese.

My brain just couldn't process that I was in the black on the balance sheet, not the red.

So, until I was confident in that, it meant I had to stick it out at my day job.

Once I had enough in my savings to hold me for a year, then I'd know it was time to stop my day job and pursue my passion, but not until then.

Not after the last four years.

Which was why I was currently crawling down the steps of the upstairs loft in my client's house.

I was a professional cleaner.

Or maid, if you wanted to get all technical and shit.

I worked for a man who I never saw, yet he always managed to make a huge fucking mess.

My guess was that he only came out at night, after I was gone.

That would certainly explain why I never saw him.

It would also explain why his house was such a freakin' pigsty every other morning when I came back.

Last night, it appeared, he'd had another party, because there were dishes and cups *everywhere*, as well as questionable things on his sheets.

My boss owned a large house on the outskirts of Dallas, right on the lake.

It was a three story monstrosity that was the bane of my existence.

But, alas, I had it clean.

For today, at least.

Now it was time to go home.

Which I did not five minutes later, being sure to lock up so I didn't get another threatening letter from my boss for forgetting.

Which I never did.

Ever.

I was a freak about locks.

I had six of them on my door at home, as well as a reinforced door, a security chain, and a half-assed security system I'd bought off of Amazon.

So yes, I understood all too well the importance of locking doors.

Something I'd found out the hard way.

Meaning I didn't screw up when it came to locking a door, especially not someone's that I had to go into where there were so many freakin' places to hide.

After locking up, I made my way home, thankful that the day's traffic was over with. Mostly.

The interstate was always busy, but it was nothing like the five o'clock rush hour.

Today, as I drove by Taco Bell and decided to get myself a burrito that I ate in the car on the way home, I was told myself that tomorrow I would start my diet.

Tomorrow I would lose the ten pounds I'd been promising to do for the last half a year.

But would it even matter if I did?

It was highly unlikely that I would find anyone.

Not unless I could meet them in traffic, at my boss's shitty big house, or at the houses where I painted my murals.

Speaking of murals, my best friend and brother from another mother, Shane, chose that moment to call.

"Hello?" I answered, pulling into my driveway.

"Why, oh why, do I not know how to paint yet?" he asked me.

I laughed.

"Because you like to work with metal," I said amusingly. "And you don't paint well."

"You like to sculpt with metal, but you can paint, too," he countered.

"That's true," I said, getting out of my car, being sure to grab the trash from my devoured burrito out of the cup holder.

I sighed and started up the front path that led to my apartment, then even further inside the building.

"What are you doing tonight?" I asked him.

"Working at the bar," he said almost distractedly. "Hey, can I call you back? I think someone's here."

He hung up before I could reply, and I sighed, dropping my phone into my purse and hitching the handles back over my shoulder.

I had no life.

Really, I didn't.

I'd worked my ass off all day, and what did I have to show for it?

Nothing.

Absolutely nothing.

No friends besides one who was a self-proclaimed workaholic and another who hated going out and doing anything, and that included spending time with me, unless she was between books.

A job that I hated.

I had nothing.

Except a dead body lying in the middle of the hallway leading to my apartment.

And a man leaning over that body.

I didn't scream, though.

No, I did something stupid. I pulled out my phone and took a picture right when his head turned.

He tensed, and it was then that I did the only smart thing I'd done in all day.

I ran.

I'd never been more thankful in my life that I only wore tennis shoes everywhere I went.

The jeans were a hindrance since they were so tight, but they didn't stop my legs from pumping or slowing me down.

Not with my heart beating ninety miles an hour and all that adrenaline coursing through my veins.

The soft curse of the male who'd been leaning over my neighbor's dead body sounded from behind me and then his heavy footsteps ate up the distance.

I ran faster.

So fast, in fact, that I ran right out of my shoe.

I didn't dare stop for it, though.

I kept going. Down the steps, out the door, and around the corner to the laundry room.

I made it through the door and got it shut and locked, eyes on the handle just in case he somehow had superpowers that made him able to open the lock without a key.

I bid him good luck. I wasn't able to do it even with the key. Which was why the residents of the building had started leaving it open for that very reason.

I kept staring at it as I backed up towards the stairs that led inside the building.

I had just made it to the steps when I felt it.

A man's—*the man's*—steely arm circled my waist, pulling me back against his hard chest.

I opened my mouth to scream but found that my vocal cords didn't work.

Mostly because the man's hand had tightened around my throat, putting pressure there and letting me know that freaking out was not the way to go right then.

My body, however, didn't get that memo.

Using my hands, feet, head and teeth, I started to thrash wildly.

My arms dug into the flesh of the man's hands.

My feet started kicking at his shins.

And my head turned to the side so I could bury my teeth in his shoulder.

His other hand came up, though, and squeezed my jaw until I had no choice but to let go of him.

And once I was free, he held my head in place and spoke softly in my ear.

"I didn't kill her," he growled. "But the man who did is still here. He hasn't left the building, so please shut the fuck up and be still."

I froze, utterly and completely.

I also don't know why I believed him, but I did.

The sureness in his voice, the complete truthfulness I could hear from that raspy dark tenor, had me believing him.

And I went limp in his arms, no longer fighting.

"Where?" I managed to squeak out.

My voice worked this time.

"I don't know," he whispered almost soundlessly. "But I need you to go into your apartment and not come out."

I started to panic slightly.

"How do you know whomever it is isn't in *my* apartment?" I asked wildly.

"Because I can see his trail," he answered, pulling me back and confusing me all at once.

He started walking, me supported in his hands now, until he'd stepped over the lifeless body of my neighbor.

"Go."

I went.

Straight to my apartment.

Where I then called the police.

***

Ian

"What happened?" the cop asked me.

I fought the urge to tell him 'none of your fucking business.' But only just barely.

Narrowing my eyes, I sent my stories into his subconscious, giving him the idea that I'd explained it all sufficiently.

The cop nodded.

"You can go. Please don't step through the crime scene again. Use the emergency stairs." He pointed to the hallway just to the side of the woman's door.

Wink.

My hand burned where I'd touched her neck earlier, and I had to also battle the urge to knock on her apartment door and demand she come with me.

At least until the fucker who'd killed her neighbor was caught.

I had a nagging suspicion that this wouldn't be the end of it. Whomever had killed Farrow's girl had done so because he knew who Farrow was.

That'd been the only impressions I could get before Wink had interrupted me with terror in her eyes as she ran from the site of the murder victim.

My eyes went down to the body of the woman again, and I had to resist the urge to place my hands on her again.

See, dead people told stories.

Not too many, but some of the people on this Earth were sensitive to ghosts.

Me being one of them.

I was what one would call a retro cognitive. Or, in layman's terms, I was able to see things that happened after they happened.

I received that gift, as well as the gift of healing, from my dragon, Mace.

Oh, My Dragon

Mace was my bonded dragon and had been since I was nineteen.

Being thirty-six now, I'd had Mace for seventeen years and would hopefully have him for many years to come.

But the fact is, there were times that I wanted to kill him just for the fact that he liked to mess with me.

He liked to make my life harder than it needed to be and, at times, it went overboard before he realized he'd gone too far.

Like now, for instance.

I was ready to go, and he was nowhere in sight.

He knew I wanted to leave.

Knew I *needed* to leave. Yet he wasn't here.

"Mace," I said through gritted teeth. "Where are you?"

If I didn't leave soon, I'd likely lose whatever patience I had left and go back up the stairs, ruining what I'd put in place by taking the woman who had made my dick stir for the first time in well over a year.

Which was why I started walking instead of staying there any longer, waiting for my wayward dragon who thought he was being funny when he wasn't.

I was about a mile away when I heard the flapping of Mace's wings from behind me.

He landed just long enough for me to sweep myself gracefully onto his back before he was up and away, heading straight for my house.

The house that, incidentally, was the same house that Wink cleaned three times a week.

I smelled her the minute I walked in the door to my domain.

She smelled sweet with a hint of flowers. Honeysuckle and vanilla to be specific.

And it was everywhere.

Before it'd just been a simple indulgence on my part.

I'd wanted her here, in my domain. I wanted her smell to permeate everything around me, stuff that I made a part of my home just to see if she'd like it.

And mostly, she did.

When I'd get home from work, I'd go over the video footage of her day. I watched her clean. Watched her sweat. Watched her cheeks become pink.

Sometimes I purposefully made my place dirtier just to see her work a little bit harder than normal.

And she always did.

My favorite days were Wednesdays because that's when she got down on her knees and scrubbed my kitchen and bathroom floors.

It was a tossup with Mondays because that is when Wink changed the sheets on my bed.

Having her scent on my sheets made me happy. Well as happy as I could be without actually having the object of that happiness in the bed with me.

I'd just slipped off of Mace, my feet meeting the spongy grass that surrounded the outside of my home, when I heard a voice that grated on my nerves.

"Where have you been?"

I swallowed hard, trying to keep my temper in check, and turned.

"Cleaning up your mess."

"Seems like you were making a bigger one rather than cleaning one up," Keifer snapped. "Why were you there?"

I crossed my arms over my chest.

"Your brother was there, and you asked me to keep tabs on him and his whereabouts, remember?" I said calmly, even though what I was feeling was definitely anything but calm.

"I wish you'd move in with the rest of us," Keifer, the King of Dragons, growled in frustration as he took a look around my house.

I didn't bother to answer him.

It was a constant battle with Keifer and me.

He wanted me to live at the sanctuary with the rest of them, but I couldn't do that.

"You know why I can't," I said.

He nodded.

"I know," he said. "It doesn't change the fact that I would like you to stay there. We're safer in numbers."

I just stared at him, and he sighed.

"Shouldn't you be with your wife and children?" I asked, hoping that'd get him to leave.

My hopes were dashed when he shook his head.

"They're at home," he said. "But my brother's not."

I nodded.

"Understandable," I said. "You know what happened?"

He nodded.

"Listened to the police scanners, and Johnson kept me updated," Keifer said. "Wanted to hear from you exactly what happened, though."

I sighed and recounted how I'd walked in on his brother, who'd been hovering over the dead girl's body.

"How did you know it wasn't him?" he questioned.

"A trail of DNA that led from the body into the apartment across the hall from hers, where the tweaker who used to call the cops on the two of them all the time lives," I explained.

Keifer's eyes narrowed.

"And the girl?" he asked.

"Which girl?" I hesitated.

There were two, after all.

"The one who got dead," Keifer said slowly, rolling his eyes like he was trying hard to contain his annoyance.

I shrugged.

"She's dead. What more do you want to know?" I asked.

Keifer rolled his eyes again.

"Why is getting information out of you like pulling teeth?" he asked angrily.

I snapped my mouth shut on the retort that wanted to burst free of my lips, barely containing my knee jerk reaction to go on the defensive at the first hint of a threat.

"She's dead. She was dead for a long time when I found her. Her murderer watched from the comfort of his peep hole as he waited for someone to find her for over an hour. I followed the fucker to the jail, then stood outside his cell, making sure his heart stopped, apparently from natural causes. Is that what you wanted to know?"

Keifer's eyes narrowed.

"You can't just go around killing humans, even if they are guilty," Keifer growled.

I turned my back on my king and then shut the door behind me.

I couldn't deal with that man anymore.

Not if he wanted me to still be a part of the team.

If that's what it was even called anymore.

My throat burned as Wink's sweet and flowery scent hit me the moment I walked through the door.

It took everything I had not to go straight to the TV and replay the day's events.

Instead, I walked to the kitchen, grabbed the bottle of whiskey that was sitting on the kitchen counter and proceeded to drink the entire fucking bottle.

CHAPTER 2

I have three moods:
1. What the fuck?
2. Are you fucking kidding me?
3. Fuck this.
-Wink's secret thoughts

Wink

The next day dawned bright and early, and I was just stepping out of my apartment when I ran into something solid.

"Oomph," I groaned.

I looked up, and my neck stretched painfully.

I'd had a rough night.

It'd started out bad due to the dead body between my apartment and me, and got worse when I had to run for my life and was caught by a beast of a man. The shitshow that was my day was capped off with me not getting a wink of sleep.

I did manage to get one hell of a crick in my neck, however.

Surprisingly, though, it wasn't because of the dead woman, but because of the sexy man who I didn't see again after I closed my apartment door on him, the one who was the cause of my sleepless night.

I cursed myself for not looking in the mirror before I'd thrown my pants on.

I was on the way to my darkroom to develop the newest shots I captured during my lunch break yesterday. First though, I had to get the processing chemicals delivered.

I'd just gotten the door open and had started to back out with the door handle in one hand and my keys in the other, when my body hit something solid.

Solid as in steel.

I turned and found myself getting lost in those same captivating eyes as last night.

"H-hey," I whispered. "Can I help you?"

He stared at me for a long couple of seconds before he blinked and his lips lifted in the barest of smiles.

This caused my heart to race and my face to flush.

Now, I wasn't so happy I'd decided to just leave instead of taking an extra five minutes to look after my appearance before exiting my apartment.

"Gosh, I'm sorry," I said, stepping back.

His eyes went down to my face and even further to my neck.

"S'okay," he muttered, his eyes focused. "You want to catch breakfast?"

I lifted my hand self-consciously and ran it along the column of my throat, surprised at the tenderness there.

Studying him, I licked my lips and began to appreciate the fine specimen of man in front of me.

He was tall and built with dark black hair and a strong jaw.

He was wearing a leather jacket and a… *scarf?*

It didn't detract from the manliness that exuded from him, however.

He was what you would think of when you thought 'male.'

Strong jaw. Jacked arms and tight abs. Dark, captivating looks. Big hands. Large feet.

The scarf, though. That was weird.

"Breakfast?" he asked again.

I snapped out of my contemplation of his manliness and shook my head.

"No," I said softly, clearing my throat. "I have to go meet the guys who are delivering my chemicals."

I had to have certain chemicals to run my photo lab, and if I didn't meet them at this ungodly hour, they wouldn't be able to get back to me until late next week. Meaning, I was up to meet them at the ass crack of dawn instead of sleeping in my nice, warm bed.

He looked at me, then nodded.

"Care if I tag along?" he asked gruffly. "Then we can get breakfast afterward?"

I bit my lip.

What the hell was going on?

This man was gorgeous. I'm talking so fucking handsome that it hurt to look at him for too long.

And his eyes. God, they were practically sucking me into his soul!

What would he want with someone like me?

I was not beautiful.

In fact, I was so far from beautiful, especially without makeup on, that I would consider myself troll-like.

Well, perhaps troll-like was exaggerating a little.

But that's what it felt like sometimes.

Especially right now.

I was nauseous as hell. My hair was in a knotted ponytail on the top of my head. My eyes had deep bags under them.

And he was everything I was not.

"Ummm," I said. "I don't…"

See, here's the problem. I didn't really know how to say 'no.'

Never had.

Which was why I ended up selling my house when my every intention had been to say 'no.'

However, the money had spoken to me, and here I was.

Which was why I said, "Sure."

He grinned and backed up, allowing me to step into the hallway.

I turned and locked the doors with my keys before dropping them into the top of my bag and zipping it up.

"Where's the house you're working from?" he asked.

I blinked.

"I told you about my house?" I asked in confusion.

I didn't tell anybody that I worked in a house. In fact, I *know* I didn't tell him.

I was already somewhat nervous around him. There was no way I would've told him where I worked.

"Last night," he said swiftly. "You were talking about it when you came up the stairs."

My mouth dropped open slightly in relief. I *had* been talking about the house when I'd rounded the stairs.

"Uh, yeah," I said. "It's on the South Side."

He blinked.

"Why'd you want to have a studio over there?" he asked curiously, offering me his hand when he started going down the stairs.

I ignored it, and instead grabbed the rickety banister that ran the length of the stairs.

Mainly because I wasn't sure if I grabbed a hold of his hand if I'd be able to let it go.

There was something about this man that affected me, and I didn't even know him.

I'd seen him a total of two times, and the first time had been under less than ideal circumstances.

Speaking of which.

"So, how did last night go?" I asked softly. "I tried to come back and see what was going on, but the cop told me to stay inside my apartment until they could clear the crime scene. I fell asleep about an hour later with all of them still stomping around in the hall."

"They found the man who did it in the apartment across the hall from yours. He was trying to burn his clothes in the kitchen sink," the man mumbled. "Apparently, he did it because she scorned him. I didn't get much before I was told to leave, too."

"What's your name?" I asked suddenly, stopping next to my old truck.

His eyes seemed to be alight with some inner fire.

"Ian. Liam Ian McHugh."

I blinked.

That was a powerful name.

"That's a cool name," I said demurely, turning my back on him to open my truck's door.

He crowded me close, and my heart started hammering.

Not because I was afraid, though, but because of his nearness.

I wanted to lean into his body about as badly as I wanted to take my next breath. Press my breasts against his solid chest.

Did I, though?

No. I managed to just barely bring my heart under control and turned my back on him, sliding into the seat of my Dually.

I was about to give Liam directions when he pushed me over, sliding my body across the seat as he moved into the driver's seat, and my ass was planted in the passenger seat for the first time in my life.

"Wait!" I said. "You can't drive my truck!"

"Why not?" he asked, taking the keys from me and finding the right one before starting it up.

"Because I don't have you on my insurance," I mumbled. "And I don't know you!"

His hand went up to his neck as he ran his fingers underneath the scarf he was wearing.

"Yet," he murmured. "You don't know me, *yet*."

I didn't bother replying.

"Where to?" he asked.

I bit my lip.

He sighed and reached for the GPS, tapping a few buttons before he made a triumphant sound and backed out of the parking spot.

"Never mind," he said, putting it into drive and pulling out into traffic. "I found it without your help."

I cursed myself.

I should know better than to leave that kind of information in the GPS. But I relied on it way too much. I was one of those directionally challenged people who rarely, if ever, was able to find her way from point A to point B without getting lost.

"Ian," I said. "I don't really know you that well. I think we should maybe start with dinner later, and go from there."

The words that left my mouth were the right ones, but what I was feeling on the inside was anything but.

"Breakfast," Ian said, mostly ignoring me and what I had to say.

"What?" I asked in confusion.

"You said dinner. And we're having breakfast," he answered distractedly. "Your truck needs to be aligned."

I blinked.

"No it doesn't. I just took it in to get aligned and had the tires rotated," I said smartly.

"You'll have to tell me who you took it to because it's obvious that whomever did it was an imbecile," he growled, pulling into traffic and merging onto the freeway. Under his breath, I could've sworn I heard him murmur 'dumbass.'

I licked my lips and tried not to stare at the way the corded muscles of his wrist bunched and shifted with each move of his arm.

Instead, I chose to fill the silence by telling him about me, out of pure nervousness rather than my wanting him to know anything more about me.

Because had I been thinking straight, likely this would've been one of those times where I realized that me telling him about myself probably was more of a turn off than a turn on.

"I'm thirty-one!" I blurted.

His eyes moved from the road to me, then back to the road.

"I'm thirty-six," he said softly.

My eyes widened.

"You don't look a day over thirty," I informed him. "But my best friend doesn't either. He could totally pass for twenty-five in a pinch. He still gets carded when we go out gambling."

"You have a brother?" he asked.

I nodded, picking invisible lint off my pants.

"Yeah," I confirmed. "He's in the Navy. I haven't seen him in almost ten years now, though."

I could feel his eyes on me, and I turned my head slightly to the left and smiled sadly at him.

"I have a sister," he said. "But she was adopted when we were younger, and I haven't seen her since."

"Have you tried to find her?" I asked.

He nodded.

"When I was younger, around eighteen or so. Stopped when I turned twenty-one," he said, turning his blinker on and leaning back in his seat.

His hand rested on the gear shift, and I let my eyes trail along the strong limb all the way up to his face.

Which was on me.

"What?" I asked.

"You aren't scared of me," he stated.

That was true.

I wasn't.

Why, I couldn't tell you.

There was something about him that made my heart feel almost light.

"There's something familiar about you," I answered him. "I don't know what it is, but I feel like I know you."

He smiled.

"You do know me," he said. "Just not officially yet."

My eyebrows quirked in confusion.

"What?" I asked. "How?"

"You work for me…kind of," he said, putting the truck into second gear as the light turned green.

I watched his feet move as I tried to make sense of his words. Then understanding dawned.

"You're…oh my God! You're the slob!" I crowed somewhat loudly.

He looked over at me with a glare as he shifted into third, then looked back to the road.

He didn't answer until he turned into the parking lot of my studio and shut the truck off.

Which was about the time I realized I'd never told him exactly where I was going. Nor did I tell him how to get there. I wasn't sure how he knew where to look on the GPS to even lead him here.

That was about the time that my psycho radar started to go off, and I remembered all those scary movies my friend Mattie made me watch when we were younger.

I'd literally just put myself into the stupid girl's shoes from my favorite scary movie. You know the one where the girl gets into the car with the sexy man, and then he drives her to a shack in the woods and shows her his doll collection made out of human skin.

I'd literally put myself into her shoes.

Of course, Ian had taken me to where I worked, not his house.

Not that he had a doll collection made out of human skin. I'd cleaned his house enough to know that he did not have one.

That wasn't to say that I was currently freaking out over nothing, though.

I moved my hand along the side of the door, feeling for the for the latch, and crowed triumphantly inside when I found it.

"Don't run," he sighed. "I knew I shouldn't have told you."

My eyes went wide when he yanked the collar at his throat and started to itch furiously.

He had a tattoo. A huge one, on his neck.

And when he saw where I was looking, he yanked the stupid scarf back into place and stared at me expectantly.

Oh yeah, I was supposed to be running.

I remembered.

Sadly, he reached out and grabbed my wrist before I could reach for the handle once again, holding me in an iron tight grip that would be next to impossible to break.

And that panic fueled my desire to get away, which set something off in me that I hadn't realized was there.

Warmth shot out of my wrist where his hand connected directly to my skin, and I pushed that energy outwards, almost as if I was forcing whatever had built up under my skin at him.

One second Ian had a hold of my hand and was tugging me toward him, and the next he was lying with his big body slumped over the front seat of my truck, dead to the world.

My mouth dropped open, and I wondered if he was playing with me.

But when I kicked him in the head in my haste to get out, he didn't move, not even to let out a groan.

He just laid there, and I wasn't sure if he was even breathing.

I stopped, just like any stupid movie girl would, and looked at him in dismay.

He hadn't actually been threatening me. He'd only asked me not to run.

I hadn't given him the chance to explain, and now he was dying because of something that I'd done to him, not that I could tell anyone what I'd done since I had no idea what it even was.

I couldn't figure it out myself.

I crept forward and started to press my hand against his head, but I froze.

Instead I picked up the old windshield wiper that was in the floorboard of my truck and poked him with it.

Nothing.

Nada.

Zilch.

The next time I poked him slightly harder and still there was no response from him.

"Sweet baby Jesus," I whispered, reaching over him into his pocket.

I found first a set of keys, and then a phone, and smiled.

Opening the phone, surprised that there wasn't some sort of lock on it, I flipped through the recent calls on his phone, choosing to go to the first person on his call list, someone who he has called more than once, a man named 'Keifer.'

The call took no time at all to connect, and five seconds after the first ring, a man answered with a terse, "You're fucking late."

"I am?" I asked.

There was silence on the other end of the line and I almost kicked myself for saying that.

"Who is this?" the man asked.

"Listen," I said, backing away from Ian. "I accidentally hurt," I choked on that word, "Ian. He's gonna need a ride."

"Where are you?" the man asked, much more tense this time. "What'd you do to him? If you hurt him in any way, I will find you, and I will make sure you suffer a fate worse than death."

"Where have I heard that before?" I muttered stubbornly. "Your threats are weak."

I got combative when I was nervous. Did I mention that before?

The man growled and I decided that was enough teasing.

"We're at a studio parking lot in the business district downtown. Corner of Lexington and Kentucky," I finally said after my senses came back to me. "I'm going to leave him propped up against the side of the building, okay?"

I hung up before he could reply, and I looked at the man slumped in my seat.

There was no way I could move him by myself, so I looked at the corner where the old man who tried to feed me every night usually stood smoking and smiled.

"Mr. Chang!" I said loudly. "Can you help me for a minute?"

Five minutes later, Ian was propped up as best as he could get against the building, and I was starting my truck and backing out of the parking lot.

After a quick wave to Mr. Chang, I peeled out of the parking lot and drove straight for the last place Ian would ever think to look for me.

His place.

It was big. He'd never find me.

I'd use the time while he was looking for me to come up with a better plan. Maybe once I could think straight, I could come up with something more plausible.

Until then, I was too fucking scared.

Plus, I had a key.

Something told me that anywhere else I decided to go, he'd find me.

If I used my credit cards or bank card somewhere, it was likely he could trace me through them.

I had to go somewhere that was free.

It was a good idea…right?

Lani Lynn Vale

CHAPTER 3

*People…not a fan.
-Ian's secret thoughts*

Ian

"Get the fuck off me," I said through clenched teeth.

Keifer stepped back and glared.

"You got yourself knocked out by a girl?" Keifer asked. "What were you doing to her? Trying to force yourself on her?"

My fists clenched in indignation.

I just stared at my king and thought about never telling him anything ever again.

So I had fucking kinky desires. So fucking what! I never did a goddamned thing without the explicit consent of the other party involved.

And just because he'd walked in one fucking time when he heard my sex partner screaming 'no' wasn't my fault. The girl had laughed when I'd been pulled off her, and she'd laughed even more when she'd explained to Keifer that it was all consensual.

That was really why I didn't live at the sanctuary with them.

Once was enough to be interrupted during sex.

"Why aren't you looking at me?" Keifer growled.

He grabbed the scarf that was miraculously still around my neck and, on instinct, I jerked away.

His hand held onto the scarf, though, exposing my neck to his gaze.

"Motherfucker," Keifer growled.

I sighed and stood up, my feet feeling like limp noodles as I backed away from him.

"Get off me," I said, lifting my hand. "You're giving me a fuckin' headache."

"Do you have your powers?" Keifer persisted.

I sighed.

"No," I answered.

"Why are you so calm about this?" he asked.

I gave him a look.

"Because it's a normal process," I answered him.

His eyes narrowed.

"How do you even know about this?" he asked. "I never told you."

I blinked in surprise.

"Do you think we're all stupid?" I asked him.

He didn't reply.

"You do, don't you?" I asked. "Well, let me tell you, we're not. We know what goes on. Everyone does. The men and women. The fucking servants. And the way y'all fight and fuck so loud doesn't help keep it a secret, either."

Keifer's face darkened to a mottled red.

"That doesn't explain how you know," he said. "And from what I remember reading, only the members of the royal blood mate. You're *not* of royal blood. I would know if I had a brother walking around out there who I hadn't met yet."

My stomach pinched.

"Psychometry," I said.

His eyebrows furrowed.

"What?" he asked.

I smiled.

"I know everything. If you've ever touched it, I know. If I want to, anyway," I said smoothly. "And honestly, I didn't really want to know this time, and I usually try to respect everyone's privacy. But I have no control over what I learn," I said blankly. "I may not be of royal blood but I have my own dragon and apparently, that's all I need to have a predestined mate."

That was my only thought.

I'd have freaked the fuck out had this happened without my knowledge.

This morning when I'd woken up and felt off, as well as later in the morning when I realized that I couldn't 'feel' anyone, I'd had a minor freak-out.

But then I remembered Keifer's mating, as well as Nikolai's. And I'd instantly calmed.

Then promptly freaked out again over the fact that I was mated.

I'd left without another thought, going straight to Wink's house to confirm my suspicions.

Last night I'd been drawn to her. But this morning, after seeing her again, it'd taken everything I had not to pull her into my arms.

And to see my mark on her neck…that'd been everything.

I wasn't even ashamed that she had my handprint on her neck.

Territorial didn't even begin to describe what I felt.

"You've been holding out on me," Keifer said stiffly.

I shrugged.

"I never signed up for anything that said, specifically, what I did and didn't have to tell you," I said, glaring at Keifer.

I was so fucking tired of being treated like I was an outsider.

I did just as much work as the rest of the fucking dragon riders. In fact, I likely did more.

Yet, not one of those motherfuckers would ever do anything for me the way they'd do it for another one of the riders.

I got up and started walking, heading for the bus stop.

If I remembered correctly, the buses ran hourly, even this early in the morning.

"Where are you going?" Keifer asked.

"The bus stop," I answered.

"Why aren't you riding Mace?" Keifer asked in confusion.

I looked over at my dragon.

"Because he pisses me off," I answered.

Keifer didn't answer, and I didn't bother to wait for him to come up with a reason that I had to stay.

I had a woman to find.

Not that it'd be very hard.

Not all of my powers left me. That, or I'd already started getting them back.

Either way I could see exactly where she went, so I could follow her very easily.

What surprised me, though, was the fact that she went to my house.

I could've guessed a thousand different places as to where she would have gone, and my place wouldn't have even made the list.

Color me fucking surprised.

***

I walked through the door and immediately noticed the difference.

Normally when Wink had been in my place, the scent of her was faint.

This time, I would've been able to tell she was here even if I hadn't known she was.

The smell of her shampoo, as well as the lotion she used, seemed to permeate the air, almost like it was circulating through my ventilation system.

It was intoxicating.

And arousing.

I didn't bother to hide my steps.

She would hear me.

She was up in the loft, and although she was trying valiantly to hide, I could see her shoes.

So, I went about tossing my shirt, seeing as it was covered in sweat, walked into the kitchen, and started cooking breakfast.

It was only nine in the morning; it was still a good time to eat.

I would have reconsidered had it been a little later.

I hated when there was that lull between breakfast and lunch, or lunch and dinner.

I never knew whether to eat or not.

Most of the time I didn't.

"You know I'm here, don't you?" she asked softly from the top of the stairs.

She was looking at me from between the slats of the landing, and I nodded absently as I grabbed a blob of butter with a spatula and plopped it down into the pan.

"How?" she asked.

"Followed your trail," I answered.

"The same one that you followed of that murderer?" she asked softly.

"Yep," I answered, reaching for the eggs.

By the time I got the bacon out of the frying pan, and all the eggs cooked, she was sitting at the bar.

"Your shirt is off," she observed.

I looked down at my chest, and then up at her face.

"Would you look at that," I said with as straight of a face as I could manage. "It is gone. Wow."

She sighed.

"I don't know what I did. But I'm sorry," she said. "You're not going to hurt me."

It was a statement, not a question.

I didn't bother to reply.

She sniffled, and I looked up sharply.

And to my horror, I saw the first tear slip down one cheek.

Another tear soon followed.

"You're crying?" I asked in outrage.

I didn't handle tears well.

There was something about them that had the power to undo me.

"You can ignore me," she said. "It's just hormones."

"Hormones?" I asked.

"You know…hormones. It's that time of the month. It just happens," she said flippantly.

"So there's no reason for the tears…you're just doing it," I observed.

She nodded.

"It happens. A lot. Sometimes I cry because I need to, like after I've seen a sad video on YouTube. Or sometimes I hear a song that I really like, and the beauty of it moves me to tears," she explained.

"So you're crying now, not because anything's amiss, but because you're a girl," I said. "Do I have that correct?"

She shrugged, causing me to sigh.

"That means nothing to me. If you're going to speak girl, you're going to have to give me a cheat guide or something. I never had a single female in my life, besides my sister, and that was a very long time ago," I told her.

She glared at me, the tears gone.

"You're not very nice," she observed.

I knew that.

I couldn't help it, either.

"I was raised in an orphanage," I said. "I have absolutely no tact. If you want hearts and flowers, you're going to have trouble getting that from me."

"Who says that I want that from you?" she challenged. "I've only known you for a very short period of time. Not even long enough to form a valid opinion of you or your character."

I sighed.

"Did you look in a mirror yet?" I asked her.

She stiffened and squirmed.

"No," she lied.

My brows rose.

"You didn't?" I asked. "Not even a little bit?"

She was cute when she lied.

Her nose had a small upturn to it, meaning I knew exactly when she started to lie because a little crease would appear on the bridge of her nose as she concentrated on what to say.

"Fine," she snarled. "What'd you do to me?"

I laughed.

"I have no fucking clue," I said honestly. "Magic, I guess."

She pursed her lips in disgust.

"Seriously?" she asked. "That's all you've got? Magic?"

I shrugged.

"I don't know what else to call it," I told her.

"Prove it," she challenged.

"I can't," I said.

"Of course you would say that. Because, why wouldn't you?" she wondered. "If I was trying to lie about how you got a tattoo that I put there, I'd lie and say it was magic, too. Although I'd have a backup plan in case you didn't fall for it."

I snorted.

"Have you ever heard of dragon riders?" I asked her.

She nodded reluctantly, sliding down onto the ledge and hooking both of her arms through the ladder that led up to the top.

"Of course I have," she answered once she was situated. "What about them?"

It wasn't often that I found someone that didn't know anything about them.

Then again, the majority of the people I came into contact with were the types who wanted to do us harm.

I was what you would call an enforcer.

The person who made sure that the dragon riders, as a whole, didn't get into trouble in any way.

If something happened, I was dispatched to take care of it.

If there was a breach at the sanctuary, I was the first one to investigate it.

Which was also another reason why I was living on the outskirts of the sanctuary and not actually in the sanctuary.

I wanted to keep my ear to the ground, and I didn't want to deal with the fucking rules and regulations that were required of me when I was living on Sanctuary land.

Such as watching the younglings.

I wasn't often in the mood to deal with them. Not because I didn't like them, per se, but because they made me wish I had those rose-colored glasses on that they did, when it came to this world.

Then there were the women who showed up whenever the fuck they felt like it. Such as Nikolai's new woman.

She was a constant pain in my ass, and she brought Keifer's woman along for the ride.

I didn't like the fact that they paid so much attention to me. It felt wrong, like my heart hurt, and I didn't want anything to do with that. When the heart became involved, things never worked out right.

Such as when my sister had been adopted and I wasn't.

I loved my sister with all my heart, and she'd been the one thing that had kept me from going crazy our first ten years together.

But then our parents had died, and instead of grieving, I had more worry piled on top of my already over-burdened young shoulders.

"You're stalling," the woman currently trying to break into my heart said.

I grimaced.

"I'm a dragon rider."

Silence followed my announcement. So much of it, in fact, that I had to stop what I was doing with the eggs and look up to make sure she hadn't fainted from the news.

She hadn't.

And she was looking at me like I'd grown a second head.

"Say what?" she asked.

I scowled at the incredulity that was tinging her voice.

"You heard me," I said. "Your eggs are finished."

She started scooting down the ladder, turning around and presenting me with her perfect ass as she maneuvered.

"How'd you know what I like?" she asked.

"You make them every day you clean here," I said. "Just figured that was the type you liked the best."

She narrowed her eyes. "That still doesn't explain how you know I like them fried, unless you've watched me."

I chose to stay silent.

"Ian..." she said. "You're not going to tie me up in the basement and torture me sexually, are you?"

I blinked.

"I don't have a basement," I said smartly, scratching my head in confusion.

"I noticed you didn't say anything about the sex torture part," she observed dryly.

I sighed.

"I'm not going to kill you. Nor harm you in any way," I told her. "You were the one who showed up at my place, not the other way around."

She didn't like what I had to say, and chose to tell me so with a glare.

I turned around to the sink to hide my laughter, dropping the pot I'd used to cook the eggs down into the sink before turning back around once I had it under control.

"This is good," she said. "Now convince me about your magic."

I pulled up my sleeves and pointed out where she'd touched me earlier.

"Look familiar?" I asked her, indicating the burn imprint of her hand.

Her lips thinned.

"Now look at your arm," I ordered her.

She reluctantly pulled up the sleeve of her shirt, and her eyes widened.

"You've turned me into a mutant!" she cried.

I sighed and leaned against the counter, eyeing her.

"I don't know where you come up with this shit," I said. "But, if you'd just give me a chance to explain before you start name calling, some of this would be solved."

She growled, and it was so cute that my cock actually twitched.

"Fine. You have five minutes before I'm leaving," she snapped.

I chose to explain, despite her bitchy attitude.

"I'm a dragon rider. I first came into my powers when I was nineteen, which was a tad earlier than most dragon riders do," I said. "My powers that I've gained from my dragon, Mace, are nowhere near what the other dragon riders have acquired."

"So, what are they?" Wink snapped.

I smiled, knowing I had her.

"Well, you used one of them on me today. Rapid energy depletion," I said.

She blinked.

"*I* used it?" she questioned.

I nodded. "Figured it out about a half second before I was out. Should've seen it coming. I knew you had my powers."

"So, what else?" she pushed.

I smiled and ducked my head so she couldn't see my lips lift.

"I can see anything that's wrong with the body and heal it. Kind of like combining an EKG, MRI, CAT scan and x-ray all in one," I continued.

She blinked at me.

"You can see what's inside me right now?" she asked.

"If I was touching you, yes," I said. "I can also see DNA outside of the body. Meaning, the other night when you asked me how I knew that guy wasn't in your apartment, I really knew. I could see his DNA trail lead in only one direction, away from the body."

"By DNA you mean…what?" she asked.

I smiled.

"Skin cells. Hair. Saliva. Semen," I said. "Not that those last two were present that night. But I could see exactly where that man went."

She nodded, her hand twisting around in her hair.

"That's kind of fantastical," she said finally, looking at me. "I'm going to take a nap. I need to think about this."

I nodded.

"There's more to tell, isn't there?" she asked as she stood.

I nodded.

"Okay," she said softly. "Tell me later."

"You know where you are sleeping?" I asked her. "Where to go?"

She looked at me like I was stupid.

"I clean this house three times a week. I think I can find an empty bedroom. Try not to trash your house while I'm not watching you," she ordered.

With that she left, leaving me with a smile on my face.

One that quickly melted away at the thought of her being in my house napping and not in my bed.

Yes, her being in my house while I was here should be fun indeed.

CHAPTER 4

It's a beautiful day to leave me alone.
-Ian's secret thoughts

Ian

"Who ate your bowl of sunshine this morning, thundercloud?" Wink's annoyingly sweet voice asked from somewhere.

"Tired," I muttered, opening my eye only enough to glare at her before closing it again.

And I was tired.

I'd spent half the night patrolling over the sanctuary, and the other half fighting with that stupid fuck, Farrow. Not to mention, when I did finally get a chance to go to sleep, thoughts of the woman two doors down from my room left me in a state I wasn't fully willing to examine.

"Are you just getting in?" she asked as she looked at me warily.

I nodded. "Patrolled."

I shuffled to my bedroom, having only gotten up two minutes before to answer a call about Farrow from Keifer.

Now I was heading back to my bed.

For at least a solid two hours. Hopefully three.

I didn't have to be at the meeting Keifer had demanded until twelve. If I went to bed right now, I'd get three hours and nine minutes.

That gave me fifteen minutes to get ready and go.

Wink had different ideas, however.

"You were supposed to talk to me this morning," she said at my back, following me into my room.

I felt her heated gaze on my back and nearly smiled when I lifted my shirt up and off my head.

She squeaked and shuffled, causing me to actually smile this time.

"What are you doing?" she asked worriedly.

"I'm getting back in bed for a few hours before I have to be at Keifer's place," I answered, starting on my belt.

My hands felt like sausages, though, as I fumbled with my belt.

I was just about to say fuck it and go to bed with them on when I felt dainty hands push mine away.

"When's the last time you slept?" she asked me, undoing my belt with comical ease.

"When you put me into a medically induced coma for two hours," I said.

She snorted.

"I thought it more of a 'passing out' on your part, rather than a 'coma' on my part," she said defensively.

I shrugged and unbuttoned my pants, thankful that they were old and worn in; meaning I didn't have to struggle to get them off.

I fell face first into the bed, rolled my head to the side only enough to set my alarm, and instantly fell asleep.

I completely missed the fact that Wink stayed in the room with me and watched my every breath for nearly ten minutes.

In fact, she'd come to check on me multiple times while I'd been asleep, something I realized within two minutes of my alarm.

I groaned and rolled over, staring up at the ceiling with bleary eyes.

I blinked rapidly, trying to clear the fog.

"You up?" she asked. "Can I go with you to wherever you're going?"

I nodded and rolled to a sitting position.

"Yeah," I muttered darkly.

She snorted and tossed something at me, and I opened my eye only enough to see it was my phone.

"What is it?" I asked.

"It's been ringing on and off for about two hours now," she said. "I took it out of here after it rang the first time. You really needed the sleep."

I glared at her.

"Thanks," I muttered dryly, rolling over and forcing feet to the ground.

My eyelids felt like they were glued to sandpaper as I shuffled my way into the bathroom.

It never even occurred to me that I was naked until I heard Wink's swift inhalation, followed by her muffled gasp.

Causing me to find my first smile that morning.

"Put some coffee on, would you?" I yelled over my shoulder.

My sides were heaving with contained laughter as I did, looking down at my dick.

I might need to tell her that I sometimes shed my clothes in my sleep.

"Mmmkay," she whispered breathlessly. "Coffee. Yes. Okay. I can do that."

She wasn't moving though, which caused me to turn around and look at her.

Her eyes immediately dropped to my crotch where my morning erection stood proud and strong.

Mostly, the erection had everything to do with her waking me up, though, and nothing to do with it being morning.

"Coffee?" I asked her.

She tore her eyes away from my cock and stared at me in complete confusion.

"Coffee?" she asked.

"Coffee," I confirmed.

She blinked, then understanding dawned as a blush stole over her face.

"Yeah. Coffee," she said. "I can do coffee."

I rolled my eyes and turned to the bathroom, slightly more awake this time.

But that slight burst of energy quickly wore off once I'd taken care of my morning wood in the shower, leaving me feeling even more drained than before.

"You really are out of it. What are you doing?" she asked, watching as I dunked another cookie into my coffee. My tenth one.

"Drinking coffee and eating a cookie. Why?" I asked.

"Is that what's always at the bottom of your coffee cups?" she asked, leaning forward to watch what I was doing.

I shrugged. "Maybe."

Honestly, I couldn't tell you if I left a mess in the bottom of my coffee cup or not. I barely ever finished the coffee.

Normally, I would get my fill on cookies and put the cup into the sink. It was rare if I ever finished it.

Even rarer if I ever washed it.

"Is it that hard for you to rinse it out once you dump it?" she asked.

I shrugged.

"I pay you to clean up after me. Why would I bother to do something so menial as that?"

She narrowed her eyes at me.

"Did you just call my profession menial?" she asked carefully.

"No," I said, standing up and taking one last sip of my coffee before I dumped it into the sink and sat the cup in the basin. "I'm calling me doing it menial. I have a hundred other things I need to be doing every morning, and rinsing my cup out is menial compared to the other things I have to do. Such as go see why the fuck Keifer's been calling me all morning."

She narrowed her eyes.

"It takes, literally, five seconds of your time to rinse the cup," she said, picking the cup up, rinsing it, and then placing it back in the sink. "It takes about ten seconds longer to place it in the dishwasher, or even better, to fucking wash it and set it out to dry in the drying rack."

I shrugged.

She narrowed her eyes.

"You're not expecting me to continue cleaning, are you?" she asked.

I stopped my forward progress to the door and turned.

"If you don't, someone else will have to come clean," I told her honestly. "So that's completely up to you."

She threw her hands up in the air in exasperation.

I turned before she could see the smile that overtook my face and started walking.

I'd nearly made it to the door when a thought occurred to me.

"You really want to come with me?" I asked as an afterthought.

Something came and went over her face, and she shrugged.

"Where are you going?" she asked.

I smiled.

"To the sanctuary," I said.

***

"This is like that place on Jurassic Park, where they kept all those birds," she said.

"The aviary?" I guessed.

She nodded.

"There's a shield surrounding the sanctuary that protects it from view, satellite and human alike," I explained, taking my own quick glance around.

Seeing it through her eyes, I could see where she got that from.

The entire place looked like it had a glass dome over it, and although it allowed anything that was supposed to be there to pass easily through it, anything that wasn't didn't get the same pass.

The grounds were large and sprawling.

There was about thirty manicured acres that the house—and I say house loosely because it was more of a mansion on steroids—sat on. On the backside of the house, there was a large pool that any of the dragon riders were free to use if they so wished it.

And then there were the dragons.

They were anywhere and everywhere.

Wherever they wanted to be, they were.

"But, I can see it," she interrupted my contemplation of the grounds.

I nodded. "You and I share a bond."

My explanation obviously distressed her.

Her mouth thinned. "I don't want to talk about it."

She fingered the handprint at her throat, and I found myself doing the same.

"We're going to have to talk about it sometime," I told her none too gently.

She shrugged.

"Then, when the time comes, we'll talk. My nap wasn't long enough to process this situation. So, for now, we're not going to talk about it. Got it?" she stated.

"Oh, snap," the thick Cajun voice belonging to Jean Luc, bawled. "She's feisty."

"Doesn't matter if she's feisty. She's an outsider. What's she doing here?" Derek, Keifer's adviser and another dragon rider, growled.

We both turned at the same time, and Derek, as well as Jean Luc, inhaled sharply.

It didn't take a genius to figure out that they'd seen the handprints on both of our throats, causing the two of them to make the connection.

"Oh, *mon loup*. You're so screwed," Jean Luc said succulently.

I ignored the both of them and grabbed Wink's hand and urged her through the door.

"Are you sure I'm allowed in here?" she asked worriedly. "They didn't look too happy to see me."

"If you weren't allowed in here, you wouldn't have made it through the shield," I muttered.

She yanked on my hand and I stopped, turning to look at her in exasperation.

"You're telling me I could've *not* made it through?" she asked.

I shrugged.

"If you weren't supposed to be here. But you're with me, so you are," I said, not understanding why she was getting so upset.

"I think you need to tell me about this bond," she said suddenly.

I sighed.

"When we get back to my place later tonight, we'll talk," I promised her.

"And where's your dragon, if you are actually a dragon rider?" she challenged.

I pursed my lips.

"Mace thinks it's funny not to be there when he knows I want him to be," I told her. "He's an asshole."

Am not, Mace's amused words drifted across my mind.

Wink gasped and said, "Who was *that*?"

"*That* was Mace," I answered. "And, like I said, he shows up on his own timetable. Sometimes not at all."

"Well, that doesn't seem very fair," she muttered. "You're not very nice."

I lifted a brow at her.

"Mace, not you," she promised, holding up three fingers for the equivalent of 'scout's honor.'

"Who are you?" a woman asked, startling us both.

I turned to find Blythe, Keifer's wife, standing there, staring at us worriedly and with more than a little bit of curiosity.

Then her eyes traveled down to our necks, and her eyes got wide.

"Oh, my God," she whispered. "You're mated!"

"Who's mated?" Keifer asked as he came into a room, a baby in the crook of his arm.

"Awwww!" Wink said. "That's the cutest baby I've ever seen!"

My eyes drifted over to Wink.

"Have you seen a lot of babies then?" I asked her.

Keifer snorted but Blythe, offended that I somehow insulted her child, huffed in annoyance.

"I'll have you know, Ian, that my child is the cutest baby I've ever seen," she insisted.

"What about your other baby?" Brooklyn, a beautiful brunette that was tall and willowy, asked.

"She is also the most beautiful. And, I like her, too," Blythe said, tossing a smile over her shoulder.

Keifer snorted.

"You just like her best because she doesn't try to tear off your nipple while she's eating," Keifer said.

"There's that, too," Blythe affirmed. "Now, are we forgetting that there's a stranger in our kitchen?"

All eyes turned to me and Wink.

Wink shrunk into my side, so far so that she hid her face behind the meat of my arm.

I moved it up and over her shoulders, pulling her into my side.

"This is Wink," I said. "Wink, the brunette with the big tits is Blythe."

Keifer hissed while Blythe blushed.

Wink pinched my side.

"Ian, that's not nice," she admonished.

I noticed she didn't disagree with me, either.

Blythe's tits, already large before, had nearly doubled in size. I was sure that Keifer was living the dream.

"Well, you do have big breasts, Blythe," Brooklyn said.

"The brunette with the long legs is Brooklyn. She's mated to Nikolai, who's likely at the helm of his computer upstairs," Ian said.

"No I'm not. I'm right here," Nikolai said, pulling his glasses off as he walked into the room and hooking them around his shirt collar. "You're new."

That was directed at Wink.

"She is," I said.

"What happened to your neck?" Brooklyn asked, coming closer.

The baby in her arms, the girl, turned her head and looked at me, and I winked.

"What was that?" Keifer asked.

"What was what?" Brooklyn asked, stopping.

"That wink you just did," Keifer said. "What are you doing, Ian?"

"Ian hasn't 'done' me yet!" Wink said indignantly. "He's been a perfect gentleman!"

I rolled my eyes skyward.

"He's not talking about you doing your man," Blythe said softly. "He's talking about that wink that just passed between Ian and my daughter."

Wink looked up at me, then back at the baby in Brooklyn's arms.

I just stared at them all blankly, not bothering to explain.

I'd perfected it over time, and I could now hold a stare with Keifer and not even blink.

I wouldn't have blinked with anybody else, but Keifer was the king after all. He expected people to bow down to his excellence and all that shit.

Me, I didn't think he was any better than the next guy.

He hadn't really proven to me that he was, anyway.

At least not to me, personally.

I respected the power he held inside of him, though, which was the entire reason I bowed down to him as the alpha and king.

If he did something to lose that respect, though, I wouldn't have any problem kicking his ass to the curb.

"You're not going to tell any of us, are you?" Blythe asked.

I smiled then.

"When she wants you to know, she'll tell you," I said.

And she would let them all know soon.

She'd relayed that information while she was still in the womb.

"That's helpful," Keifer muttered. "Your psychological bullshit isn't needed right now, Ian."

"Then why did you ask me to come over here for a meeting?" I asked, shrugging and turning to leave.

Wink held on to my hand like a landline, following closely behind me without me even telling her to do so.

"Stop," Keifer said. "I did have a reason for asking you over here."

I sighed and turned, leaning my back against the wall beside the backdoor.

"So get it over with. Ask me," I ordered.

Keifer's eyes narrowed.

"You do realize that I'm the King here, right? If I want to take all day, I can damn well take all fucking day," Keifer growled in annoyance.

Wink's hands tightened on my forearm as she read the hostility in the room.

Good. She would need to pay fucking attention if she was going to be with me.

And she would be with me.

Not only had fate made it so, but I'd wanted her for so fucking long I couldn't even begin to count the days.

It'd been two years and some odd months since she'd started cleaning my house, and I'd known for at least a year that she was my mate.

I'd let her be, though, knowing she'd be safer away from me.

As long as I didn't touch her, we'd be okay.

And then, in a freak meeting, she'd shown up where she shouldn't have been, and all my training had deserted me.

I'd touched her. Stolen her life from her with one single touch, and she didn't even know it.

I could have stayed away. Should have. But the moment I saw her up close and personal, I knew fate had intervened.

"I realize that," I rumbled, squeezing my arm into my side and giving Wink a reassuring squeeze when she started to tremble.

The power in the room had grown exponentially since I'd arrived.

Which was why I never stayed longer than I had to.

The longer Keifer and I were in the same room, the more the tension built until something broke.

Usually, it was me…or something that belonged to me.

But this time, that wouldn't be happening. This time, I had Wink to protect.

And Keifer saw that I wasn't going to bend. Not this time, anyway.

So he got on with what he wanted me there to talk about.

"Blythe, will you please tell Derek and Jean Luc to come in here?" Keifer said on a put-upon sigh.

Blythe's eyebrows rose in surprise. "Where are they?"

"They're in my office," Keifer said.

"I'll go with you. I have to go throw up," Brooklyn said as she passed the baby she was holding to Keifer then left the room.

Wink's hand tightened on my arm, and I looked down at her.

"What?" I asked.

"She's having a boy." Wink muttered softly. "Why do I know that?"

I smiled.

"You can see their DNA," I told her. "That's part of my powers that I share with you now, remember?"

Nikolai's startled exclamation had both of us looking up before Wink could reply.

"What?" Wink asked. "Did I say something wrong?"

Everyone was staring at us, including Derek and Jean Luc who'd come in through the back door.

"What do you mean, she's having a boy?" Nikolai asked.

"You never told me what I was having," Keifer said.

Did I detect a note of hurt in his voice?

Surely not.

"That was because you never asked," I said distractedly, my head turning slightly. "Why did you tell her to go get Jean Luc and Derek if you could summon them through mind speak? And why did you send her in the wrong direction when you knew that they were outside?"

Keifer's eyebrows rose.

"I'm still trying to wrap my head around the fact that I'm having a boy. Do you think he'll be as big as me?" Nikolai asked.

We all stared at him.

"Not when he's born," Wink said nicely. "Maybe when he grows up, though."

Nikolai's mouth turned up at one side in a grin. "That's good to know."

"Can we get on with what we came here for?" I asked, annoyance clear in my voice. "I haven't had but a few hours of sleep."

Keifer's eyes narrowed.

"Why not?" he asked.

"Because I was on duty last night, like you asked me to be. Remember?"

Keifer shrugged.

"And then I had to go talk to a guy about some things," I said.

"What things?" Keifer asked. "Who?"

Farrow chose that moment to come into the kitchen, and he looked bad.

My mouth kicked up at the corner at seeing the job I'd done on him.

Twice.

He deserved it.

Farrow was the most selfish motherfucker on the planet, and if my opinions held any clout with Keifer, I'd recommend that the little fucker find someplace else to live.

He was going to get us all in trouble.

Had gotten us all in trouble.

A lot.

But the little fucker was royalty, and Keifer's brother.

So, no matter what I thought, Keifer would never kick Farrow to the curb.

Farrow would likely be on Keifer's tit for the rest of his life.

"What happened to you?" Keifer asked Farrow.

"Nothing," Farrow said, his eyes sliding to me once before turning back to the cabinet where he was reaching for a cup.

I turned my eyes back to Keifer, my eyesight offended that I'd chosen to look at Farrow as long as I had.

The motherfucker really got on my nerves, and it chapped my ass every damn day that I ever got into the situation that I needed help from him.

"You'll tell me later when we're alone," Keifer ordered his little brother.

I snorted, causing all attention to come back to me.

Wink squeezed my hand, letting her small fingernails dig into my skin.

CHAPTER 5

Book sniffing (verb): breathing in the scent of a book, sometimes in secret.
-Wink's not-so-secret secret

Wink

I was so goddamned lost it wasn't even funny.

Everyone kept casting me furtive glances, most of them filled with pity.

In fact, it was happening so often that I wanted to yell at them.

I didn't know what that was all about, or why they were doing it, but I was seriously at the point where I was about to lose it.

And I really hated the way nearly all of them sounded like they were talking down to Ian with each word that came out of their mouth.

The bigger brother was fighting with the little brother, that I could tell from what little information I knew.

The weird thing was how I knew they were brothers.

I could see their DNA. It was like it was floating in the air around them.

A whole bunch of letters like I saw in science class during college.

They were wrapped around each man like a second skin, and I had to resist the urge to go over there and see if I could move the letters by pressing on it.

"You'll tell me when we're alone," the big man said to the little man.

Then Ian snorted, and I squeezed his hand when all eyes came back to him.

"Do you have something to add to this conversation?" Keifer asked through gritted teeth.

"No," Ian said, no apology whatsoever in his tone.

Kiefer turned more fully to Ian, giving his brother his back.

"How about you enlighten me about what was so funny, then?" Keifer said slowly.

Derek, Nikolai, and the accented one—Jean something or other—all looked warily between the two men.

I shifted, putting myself even further into Ian's hold, something in which Keifer caught.

"Maybe we can discuss this in private," Keifer suggested, his eyes going to me and then back to Ian.

"Keifer!" Blythe called. "Can you get someone to bring the babies to me? It's time for them to eat."

My eyes went to the two babies who were asleep and clearly not hungry, otherwise they'd be letting people know.

Nonetheless, Keifer sighed and turned to walk out the door.

"Fucking pussy," Farrow, the unwise brother, said to Keifer's back.

Keifer froze, and then turned to glare at his brother.

The baby in his arm, jostled by the movement, woke.

"Take the baby," Keifer said, handing the baby off to Pierre or whatever the hell his name was.

Pierre promptly passed the baby to Derek, who then looked at me like I would know what to do with him.

I rolled my eyes, loosened my hold on Ian, and held out my arms.

Derek handed the baby over, who stared not at me, but at Ian.

"Why's this kid staring at you like you know all?" I whispered to Ian.

Tell you later, he said in my head.

My eyes widened in alarm.

Nikolai, the other brother, came over to me with the other baby, and placed her into my other arm without me even saying he could.

"Go up the stairs once you exit the kitchen. First door on your right is the nursery," he said.

I looked over to Ian who nodded his assent, and I blinked.

"O-okay," I said. "I'll be back."

"Wait until he comes and gets you," Keifer growled at me.

I turned and stared at him with annoyance.

"How about I come down here when I feel like it, hmm?" I asked nastily. "And how about you stop being so mean."

His eyes narrowed, and Ian growled before Keifer could say what I could see at the tip of his tongue.

"Go, Wink," he said softly.

I went, but only because the babies in my arms were starting to wake up and whimper.

"Y'all are just the cutest things I've ever seen," I cooed at them. "But don't tell my clients that. They think their babies are the cutest."

Neither kid had anything to say to that, and I chose to ignore the intelligence I could see lingering in their young eyes.

I also ignored the fact that I was walking in someone's house that I didn't know. Nor did I feel like I belonged.

The fact that Ian didn't seem to 'belong' either, didn't help my feelings much.

I could sense an underlying current of hostility from the entire room, and it was quite disconcerting to know that it was directed at Ian.

He may not be the nicest of men, nor the chattiest, but he was actually a pretty good guy.

He made sure to always give me a bonus around the holidays. A generous one.

He paid me triple what I got at my other jobs, and he always made sure to stock the kitchen and fridge with my favorite food and drinks when I was there.

Not many men I knew stocked flavored water bottle mixes for no other reason than their maid liked to drink that when she came over to clean.

"Oh!" Blythe said as she came hurrying out of the room. "I wasn't sure if they heard me yell."

I gladly relinquished one of the babies to her, following her into the room where she immediately took hers over to a changing table.

Then I watched in fascination as she chatted and changed the baby's diaper.

"You're mated to Ian. That's so cool," she said as she reached for the wipes. "I never thought he'd find someone with that whole 'back off' vibe that is always wafting off of him."

"What do you mean?" I asked her, placing the baby in my arms onto the changing table once she'd finished with hers.

She then passed me the baby she held, and I took a seat in the rocking chair opposite of the padded glider and waited patiently for her to finish.

"Do you mind if I breastfeed with you here?" she asked. "I'd like to tell you a few things."

I blinked, then nodded my head.

"Sure," I said. "I don't mind."

Then she proceeded to the second rocker to feed the first baby under a cover as she spoke to me about Ian, telling me some interesting things I'd yet to learn about him.

"He saved all of our lives," she said. "When I was pregnant with these two, some things happened that hurt Nikolai, his sister, me and Brooklyn," she winced slightly and shifted her stance before continuing. "And he was the one there to nurse us all back to health."

"Oh," I said with a smile as I looked down at the little baby in my arms. "I'm sure he just loved that. He's so private and hates being in crowds."

"How do you know that?" she asked, her eyes sharpening.

My brows furrowed.

How did I know that?

Memories.

I blinked.

What? I asked him.

My memories. You have them. You have everything you want of mine. We share our powers, so all you have to do is touch something of mine and you'll get whatever you want from it. Sometimes it's not something you're aware of getting, either, he whispered into my mind.

You're telling me I can touch anything I want and get whatever memories associated with it that I want? I wondered.

Yes, he said. *Just touch the nearest object. Concentrate on it. It'll show you the memories associated with it.*

My eyes went to the bed, and then I shivered thinking about what might've happened on that bed, so I chose to go with the chair that I was sitting in.

And I got a full, firsthand show of absolutely everything that had ever gone on in that chair.

Starting with the newest imprint, which happened to be a snippet of Keifer and Blythe kissing with the babies in Blythe's arms. Then it moved on to Blythe rocking in the chair, watching the cribs with longing in her eyes.

Then it transformed.

Into something so naughty that I had to pull away with a gasp.

"Oh, my God," I whispered, the scene replaying in my mind, only I had a front row seat to what had happened.

"Keifer please," Blythe whispered. "Fuck me."

Keifer growled and dropped down to his knees, his eyes staying on mine as that long, wicked looking tongue darted out of his mouth and licked my pussy.

His tongue circled my clit, round and round.

His hand smoothed up my thigh, and my fingers dug into the smooth, cool wood.

"Wink!" Blythe called loudly. "What's wrong? Did the baby show you something?"

I blinked, surprised.

"What?" I asked, a blush stealing up over my face. "No, your baby didn't show me anything."

"Then what did you see?" she asked. "Jean Luc told me that my baby boy can project his thoughts into anyone he wants to. He thinks it hasn't happened yet since he's still so young, but Jean Luc can feel his latent powers."

"Jean Luc can tell the baby already has powers?" I asked. "Ian told me that dragon riders were around twenty-one years of age before they came into them."

"They are," Blythe nodded in confirmation. "But my boy is the future king, and there are powers and entities, as well as prophecies galore, swirling around right now that were never here before. My husband has two theories. One, it's only because my son's the future King and he came into contact with his dragon in utero. Two, something is happening that is waking their powers up earlier."

"Are there any more children who are exhibiting these powers?" I asked curiously.

"Not that we are aware of," Brooklyn said as she came in and collapsed on the bed. "I hate throwing up."

I looked at her, and the DNA that seemed to swirl around her. One set of DNA was most definitely hers. But the other, no. The other was not hers. That I could tell almost immediately. But it was also a part of her. Part hers, and obviously part the man, Nikolai, from downstairs.

It was so amazing to see this that I stared at her for so long that she shifted uncomfortably.

"I'm sorry," I said. "There's just something about you that's intriguing."

She blinked.

"Like what?" she asked curiously.

"Ian's told me a little bit about his powers, but apparently, I'm able to see DNA. And it surrounds everyone like an aura. But I have to concentrate to see it," I explained. "With you…I don't."

"What do you mean?" she asked, leaning back onto two elbows in the bed.

"I can see the DNA of your son wrapped around you like a coat…or whatever," I said, running my hand in the air around her. "It's freaking cool."

Her mouth dropped open in surprise.

"Son?" Blythe asked in surprise.

"Son?" Brooklyn parroted.

I nodded. "Yes. Son."

CHAPTER 6

Just when I think stuff is looking up, life bitch slaps me and reminds me that it's not.
-Ian's secret thoughts

Ian

"What did my daughter say to you?" Keifer growled in frustration. "And what the hell is going on with you and my brother?"

I looked over at Farrow, wondering if he was going to address this, but he looked away to stare out the window.

I sighed.

"Your brother's a fucking dumbass who tried to buy drugs from his girlfriend's neighbor," I said. "And when your brother brought the freaky fucker's attention to the girl, the girl got dead because your brother liked to fuck her in the hallway."

Farrow's fists clenched.

"Guy didn't much like the object of his obsession getting fucked in the hallway, so the next time he saw her there alone, he killed her because she was a 'slut', according to him," I continued, watching Farrow's face as I explained.

Keifer stiffened, and Nikolai growled in frustration.

"Seriously, Farrow?" Nikolai surprised me by being the one to speak. "Drugs? Is that what it's come down to?"

Farrow stiffened even more, turning to look at his brothers.

"You don't know what it's like," he said. "I can't stop the voices. They're killing me."

"Do you think we all harnessed these fucking powers in a day?" Keifer asked in a deceptively calm voice. "We didn't. In fact, I still learn new fucking things every fucking day, yet you don't see me turning into a little bitch and using drugs when I'm faced with difficult and complex situations or problems. And, by the way, little brother, I'm faced with those kinds of problems every hour of every fucking day."

Farrow shrugged.

"Don't know what to tell you. I'm not you," he said. "And thanks to him, I now have to figure out an alternate path."

"What do you mean by 'thanks to him?'" Keifer asked, glancing at me before returning to Farrow.

Farrow looked at me in disgust.

"He fucking fucked with my goddamn brain, and now every time I even think about drugs, I get a splitting headache that brings me to my knees," Farrow said.

Nobody said anything, and I had a feeling that they agreed with my methods.

They may not like that they did, but they were appreciative nonetheless.

Keifer sighed.

"Fucking wonderful. At least something's going our way today," Keifer muttered.

His gaze swept back to me and he crossed his arms.

"Now, tell me what that was that passed between you and my daughter earlier," Keifer ordered.

I sighed and turned to look out the window.

"Nothing happened or 'passed' as you say," I said. "I can just read her. I know."

"You know what?" Keifer asked tiredly.

"That she dream walks. Your son isn't your son…"

CHAPTER 7

I was asked why I use the f-bomb so much. I replied with, "What the fuck is an F-bomb?"
-Why Ian can't be taken to nice places

Ian

The moment Kiefer's hand smashed into my face, I was running.

Not because I was scared of Keifer, but because the motherfucker had hit me.

And whatever happened to me was now transferred to my mate.

My mate.

Even the words sounded foreign to me, but it was what it was.

I hit the stairs at a dead run, wiping blood away from my nose as I went.

It kept pouring out, so I ignored it in favor of concentrating on the steps.

I was glad I did as I came up to the last one and found Wink lying at the top of them, unconscious from the psychic blow she'd just received.

Keifer's fist slamming into my face had hurt like a motherfucker, but it'd only stunned me for seconds at most.

Keifer's punch straight to Wink's face, psychic as it was, was not only enough to stun her, but it'd knocked her out cold.

"Wink," I whispered, dropping down to my knees on the top step and bending over so I could run a scan.

Placing my hand on her cheek, I closed my eyes and let my mind drift out of my own body and into hers.

Doing this left me vulnerable, but I knew I was safe here among the dragon riders, despite the fact that Keifer had just punched me in the face, and essentially, my mate.

He hadn't thought through the consequences of his actions, otherwise he would've never hit me, which, in turn, hurt Wink.

That didn't mean I didn't want to punch the shit out of him.

But I, at least, thought about the consequences of my actions.

Meaning I didn't beat the shit out of the motherfucker like I wanted to do.

Badly.

"Shit. Fuck," Keifer said from the stairs behind me.

I didn't bother answering him as I finished my scan of Wink's body.

The only damage I could find was to her face, and that was only superficial.

I didn't leave her where she was.

Instead, I picked her up, turned on my heel and moved down the stairs.

Keifer wisely moved out of my way, but I still flayed him alive with my glare as I walked past.

"Ian," Keifer said softly. "I'm sorry."

Sorry wasn't good enough.

I didn't bother to reply, walking past everyone that stood watching me without a word, straight out the door.

For once in his life, Mace was where I needed him to be—right outside the door.

Guess I'd be leaving my bike here in a safe place instead of on the side of the road when Mace finally deigned to grace me with his presence.

"Thank you, Mace," I said gruffly, walking up to him and mounting his back with practiced ease.

Mace took off without another word, and I used my legs to hold myself on Mace's back as we flew back to my property.

He landed in the backyard just as Wink was rousing.

She moaned and tried to turn, which only brought her deeper into my arms.

She snuggled deep and sighed, her eyes fluttering open slightly before they slammed back closed.

"The sun," she whined. "It burns!"

I laughed and slid off of Mace's back, going up to my door and pressing my thumb against the scanner.

It read my fingerprint and immediately opened.

"My face hurts," she said, twisting slightly.

Her eyes opened once we were in the darkness of the kitchen, and she stared at me in confusion.

"You have blood all over you," she whispered, pain filling her voice.

"You do, too," I said, taking her to the kitchen counter and dropping her on her bottom next to the sink.

"What happened?" her voice cracked, as well as her jaw, as she asked that.

I winced, turning to face her fully.

"I forgot to mention something this morning," I said.

Her brows rose.

"Okay," she drawled. "How about you tell me as I clean your face."

Her eyes studied my face, and I pushed her hand away before she could grab the washcloth.

"No," I said. "You'll let me do you first. Listen as I clean."

She rolled her eyes.

"I bet that's the first time you've ever said that," she said cheekily.

I started to clean her face as I spoke.

"I told you about the powers we acquire from our dragons. What I forgot to mention was that when you and I bonded, you also acquired the ability to feel what I feel. Whether that be happiness, excitement, anger. Or pain."

She blinked.

"Pain?" she asked.

I nodded.

"These tattoos," I dragged my finger across her neck. "They do more than just show everyone that you belong to me."

"What else do they do?" she asked warily, her eyes scanning my face.

I threw the washcloth into the sink, which she promptly picked up and turned back to me. This time she cleaned me up.

"When I feel pain, you feel pain. Such as when Keifer slammed his fist into my mouth about ten minutes ago, it not only affected me, but you as well," I informed her.

"What about when I have my period?" she asked. "Or when I have a baby. Will you feel that pain, too?"

I was shaking my head before she finished, trying to will my heart to slow upon hearing 'when I have a baby', and said, "No. Anything that your own body does to you, will stay with you. Such as if I acquired cancer and died, you would feel none of that pain that was directly involved with it. I would be very aware that you were going through childbirth or cramps, but I wouldn't necessarily have to feel everything."

She shivered.

"Cancer sucks."

I nodded.

"It does," I agreed.

"My dad died of cancer," she said.

I knew, but I didn't want to let on that I did.

I'd had her thoroughly investigated before I'd allowed her to come into my home. In fact, I'd had her investigated so deeply that I knew that she sucked at science, but excelled greatly at art, and music in high school and had actually taken up photography while still in school.

She was also dyslexic, something I'd found out when I had Nikolai hack into her school records.

That was something I was fairly sure she wouldn't want me to know, at least not yet.

Likely not anytime soon, either.

"I'm sorry. So did my parents," I said softly.

Her eyes widened.

"Both of them?" she gasped.

I nodded.

"How is that even possible?" she questioned.

I shook my head.

"Not really sure, to be honest," I explained. "My mom got ovarian cancer. She seemed to be beating it, but then my dad was diagnosed with pancreatic cancer about eight months after we found out about my mom," I looked at the wall behind Wink's head as I said the next part. "My dad's cancer was advanced. There was nothing the doctors could do when they found out. He died about five months after he was diagnosed, and the last three of them, he was bedridden."

"And your mom?" she prodded gently.

"Died about five months after my dad. Mom was still going through her treatments and by the time his end came, they were so far in the hole financially, that she just stopped them altogether," I answered. "We were really poor. My sister and I got our clothes at Goodwill on the good days, and on the bad we just wore the same outfit over and over again, despite the fact that they didn't fit." I cleared my throat and looked at her. "It was bad. When my mom died, my sister and I were split up into different homes."

Her eyes showed sorrow.

"That's terrible," she said. "Have you ever found her?"

I nodded.

"Found her. Then let her go without seeing me," I said. "Haven't actually seen her with my own two eyes since college."

Wink's eyes filled with tears at that explanation, but before she could finish the question I could see in her eyes, I pulled out the bag of peas from the fridge and placed them on her face.

Her gasp had me smiling, and the one eye I could see of hers had me wanting to laugh.

"Why did you get hit?" she asked, changing the subject.

"I told Keifer his son wasn't really his son," I said honestly.

Her eyes widened.

"How do you figure?" she asked. "How can one baby be his, and the other baby not be?"

"I didn't mean it like that," I said. "I was talking about another kid."

Her brows furrowed. "What does that mean?"

I sighed and picked her hand up to hold onto her peas, and then started pacing.

"I don't know," I said. "I touched something a few months ago when I was investigating a cabin where Brooklyn had been held, and I saw something that I haven't been able to make sense of. And each time I focus on it, all I get is confusion, and the repeated words 'your son isn't your son.'"

She waited for more, but when I didn't give it to her, she opened her mouth to reply.

"And did you tell that to Keifer?" she asked.

I shook my head.

"No," I said. "I was trying to tell him more when he took offense to me implying that his son wasn't really his son, and punched me."

She shook her head.

"Why would he know to ask you about that anyway?" she asked.

"The wink I gave the girl," I said.

"Do they have names?" she asked. "And why did you wink at her? Isn't she like a week old?"

I nodded.

"Grace and Reed," I said. "And they're two weeks old. As for why I winked at her, the babies are intelligent creatures. They're very aware of what's going on around them, and the girl—Grace—and me bonded."

"How?" she asked.

I studied her for a long moment, before shrugging and explaining.

"She's a dream walker," I said. "She can leave her body like Nikolai and his woman can, but only during sleep. She does this almost nightly, and for some reason keeps finding me in my sleep. She keeps repeating the same thing to me that I saw when I was in that cabin. 'Your son isn't your son.'"

"That's the weirdest thing I've ever heard," she said. "What do you think it means?"

I was shaking my head before she'd finished.

"I'm not sure. I have no clue who it's about, or why I would be the one to keep hearing and seeing it," I said. "My ability to see people's pasts through objects is normally very definitive. I can usually pick up anything I want. But what I got from picking up that lamp was nothing in comparison to what I usually see. It's as if the person that touched it, who it belonged to, was gifted as well, and was able to shield most of his memories."

She pursed her lips.

"Did you try going back, seeing if you could pick something else up?" she asked.

My brows went up in surprise.

"No; actually, I never really thought about it," I answered. "But now that you mention it, I can go back. The cabin is now owned by Vassago properties. It hasn't been touched since it happened."

"Well, let's go!" she insisted, jumping up and causing the peas to drop to the ground.

I bent and picked them up, and then walked to the freezer and tossed them back inside.

"You're not going with me," I said. "But I will go."

She looked at me with a small pout tipping the corners of her lips down, and I sighed.

"Fine," I said. "But if I tell you to do something, you listen to me or we're out of there."

She curled her lip up at me.

"Fine," she said.

"Fine."

CHAPTER 8

*How do I like my eggs? In cake.
-Every woman's secret thoughts*

Wink

"Oh, my God! We're going to die!" Wink screamed, covering her face with her hands.

I refrained from asking her what she thought she was going to accomplish by doing that, but only just barely.

I sighed when Wink started to scream louder as Mace went a little sharper in than she was expecting.

"Jesus!" I said, slapping Mace's flank. "She's new to dragon riding!"

Mace's dark chuckle rose up, and it let me know that it wasn't just me that Mace liked to torture. I was sure he liked to torture children and small animals as well.

I hopped off, falling the six feet or so to the ground, and then held my hands out for Wink since Mace didn't like getting his knees dirty by bending down.

Fucker.

I heard that, Mace said with amusement.

You were meant to, you rude jackass, I thought to him.

"This is a nice area," she said as Mace lumbered off toward a crop of trees across the clearing from the small cabin.

"It is," I said. "I bought it through Vassago Industries."

"You bought it?" she asked. "Why?"

I shook my head. I didn't know why I bought it. I just did.

Something about the area called to me, but I couldn't quite put an exact reason behind the urge.

I looked around the area, trying to see it with a new idea.

It really was nothing special.

In fact, it was just a cabin in the woods. Trees lined all four sides, and the only clearing in the entire area was the lawn in front of the cabin.

Hell, Mace couldn't even land anywhere near the house unless he wanted to do it on the roof—which was showing signs of wear where other dragons had landed and done damage before. He had to land about five hundred yards away, near the pond, and we had to walk to the cabin due to the thickness of the trees.

The trees themselves looked to be about two hundred years old, and I doubted with even the smallest of ones I would be able to get my arms wrapped around the trunk.

"Why are you looking at the trees like that for?" Wink asked me curiously, staring at the same tree I was.

"I was wondering if I'd be able to wrap my arms around it and touch," I said instantly, not afraid to unshield my thoughts from her.

She walked up to the tree and leaned into it, wrapping her hands around it and not coming close to touching her fingertips.

I stared at her for long moments, my eyes automatically going to her jean clad ass.

My dick started to harden, and I swallowed as I closed my eyes and forced myself to move.

I walked past her to the cabin, knowing if I didn't I'd turn her around and slam her back into that tree, then tear her pants from her body before filling her up with my cock.

I didn't know what it was about Wink that turned me into a monster, but just the sight of her hugging a fucking tree had me hard as a rock.

"Hey!" she said, affronted that I would leave her behind. "Wait up!"

I slowed my pace for her to catch up, and covertly readjusted my cock in my jeans before she arrived at my side.

"So, tell me about you," she ordered as we walked.

I looked over at her, my eyes taking in the way her blonde hair seemed to glow blue in the sunlight.

"What do you want to know?" I asked roughly, turning back forward.

"What's your favorite color?" she asked.

"Red," I said instantly. "What's yours?"

"Magenta," she answered just as quickly.

I looked over at her.

"Purple?" I tried.

She shook her head.

"No. Magenta," she corrected me. "Where did you grow up?"

"Here in Dallas," I said. "Then I went to an orphanage and was in and out of foster homes until I was eighteen."

She looked at me curiously, a weird gleam in her eyes that I couldn't quite read.

I arrived at the steps and held out my hand to offer support as she climbed them.

The cabin wasn't in the best of shape, and a stiff wind would likely blow the whole damn place down with the next rain storm we got.

"Magenta is my favorite color to see through the lens of a camera."

"That makes sense, I guess," I said to her. "I saw your photos at the gallery downtown. They're beautiful. And your sculptures are pretty awesome as well; although I'm not sure how I feel about you getting that close to fire and liquid metal."

She looked over at me in confusion.

"How did you know I had photos in a gallery?" she asked, her eyes narrowed.

"Had you investigated," I answered truthfully. "What did you think? I was just going to let some random stranger into my house?"

She pursed her lips.

"You could have asked my permission to do it first," she muttered under her breath as she reached for the door handle.

I stopped and watched as her hand first touch the cool metal door handle.

Her eyes went hooded, and her pupils dilated as she got her first reading on the old cabin.

There was a lot there.

A family of four had built the place in the early 1900's; the parents had died, leaving the kids alone at the ripe young age of sixteen. From there, the eldest sibling had lived there with the sister until the sister had died of pneumonia two years later.

The memories continued through the brother's life, all the way up until he walked in one last time in the nineteen eighties and never came back out alive again.

The next time someone had entered the cabin had been when three men had come out there around a year ago and started fixing it up.

I watched, and waited, for Wink to get all the memories that I did from the door handle.

Sometimes they had to be searched for, but the ones on the door handle were so complete that I doubted she would have to.

Which she told me not ten seconds later.

"That was amazing!" she said excitedly. "Why don't I have to do that everywhere?"

I explained the basics to her, and she nodded.

"So this is all the time for you?" she asked, pushing the door open.

I nodded.

"I've gotten to the point where the images and information cycle into my mind, into a different compartment than my normal thoughts take place," I said, walking through the door behind her and turning on the light. "You'll get to that point too, I'm sure. You've already partially taken on my habits, at least when it comes to the powers. You know me, and when you learn something new by touching something of mine, you process it and forget about it almost as fast as it happens. Kind of like the DNA. I see it but I don't 'see it.' Not unless I'm actively telling my brain to process the information."

"Hmm," she said, looking around the room.

There wasn't much to the inside just like the outside.

It was a one-bedroom open styled floor plan. One side of the large room was the kitchen, where we were currently located. The other side housed a bed and wardrobe, as well as a bathroom behind a curtain.

The single window that led to the outside was worn and needed to be thrown away and replaced.

The lighting, however was atrocious. The lamps that were inside were dull, and barely lit the room.

But one of the benefits I'd acquired from Mace was sharper than normal eyesight.

I could see in the dark, which meant that Wink could see in the dark now, too.

Something that she realized when she headed into the room and automatically walked to the string that would turn the light on.

"I can see in the dark," she said, sounding only mildly surprised.

"Yep," I confirmed.

"I wanted superhuman strength," she said.

I snorted.

"So did I," I said. "But, as you can see, I only get what I'm gifted with. Alaric, one of the other dragon riders who you haven't met yet, has strength like you're speaking of. He can do just about anything strength wise, but that's all he can do."

"Hmm," she said. "I'll have to weigh the benefits."

She looked around the room while I walked up to the table that Brooklyn had been tied down to, and placed my fingertip on it.

It was a hack I'd grown accustomed to using when I was wary of seeing something that might overwhelm me.

When I was younger and still trying to control my powers, I'd learned to be careful about what I touched, because if I wasn't, I'd be lost in the memories without my conscious desire to do so.

I'd had to come up with an adaptive technique in the instance that I needed to be aware of my surroundings, but also needing to read something.

The less skin that's touching the object you're trying to read, means the less information dump you get.

Doing it the way I did it with the fingertip meant I could control how fast the memories came at me so I could pay attention as well.

Wink watched me work, then did the same thing I was doing.

"Force the memories into your box," I instructed. "Form the box with your mind, and then funnel them into the box, but also pay attention to me at the same time. Okay?"

She pursed her lips and watched me.

"Working?" I asked her.

She nodded.

"What do you see?" I asked her.

"Pain. Brooklyn. She was in pain," she whispered.

I nodded.

"Her brother. That's the male you see in the picture. He teamed up with the purists—religious zealots that didn't think anything but humans should live on Earth—and tried to lure Nikolai here using Brooklyn," I informed her.

She nodded.

"I can see," she confirmed. "There's another male in the background, but I can't get a sense of him."

I nodded.

"That's the man I think can hide his aura. His signature," I said. "I can feel him, too, but I can't get a definite identity on him like I can with everyone else."

She picked her hand up and walked to the chair in the corner, following the same process I'd just showed her.

I followed her lead and started touching random objects as well, but ended up with the same results each and every time.

"Damn," Wink said. "I was really hoping you'd get something."

I nodded my head and walked to the door, opening it for her.

"I have to go on patrol within an hour," I informed her. "I need to get you home."

"Patrol?" she asked. "Do you do that every night?"

I nodded my head and switched the light off as I walked outside, closing the door behind us as we left.

"I do," I confirmed. "Usually it's more equally split within the ranks of the dragon riders, but Alaric, Ford, and Dorian have been sent to separate areas to protect them from a possible threat, and haven't been back to share the burden."

"Ouch," she said. "Why do they need to protect the other places?"

"There are six hearts spread out over the United States; each heart contains the life force that the dragons need to stay alive. Each dragon has to stay within two hundred square miles of each heart, or they'll start to age like any mortal being," I explained. "We have to protect these places, otherwise our dragons could die off, and in turn, so could we."

"What exactly do you mean by 'heart?'" she asked, reaching for the hand I offered her.

Hand in hand, we both walked to where Mace was eating apples off a nearby tree.

"The heart is what I would call an 'energy field'," I explained. "It gives the dragons the fuel they need to fly and perform their special abilities. We also found out, not too long ago, that the heart could also heal. It healed Nikolai when he was hurt and Brooklyn took him there. It also healed Blythe when she lost too much blood after having the twins."

"Oh," she said. "Brooklyn and Blythe explained a little about what happened today while I was up in their room. Just before…you know." She pointed to her eye.

My teeth ground together.

"What?" I asked, running my fingers over the raised tattoo.

"I found something out this afternoon, and I've been trying to work up the courage to ask you about it," she blurted.

I blinked. "Okay."

"It's about this," she said, fingering her own neck now. "The ladies told me a few things about the tattoos, and they said ours were different than theirs."

She licked her lips with nervousness.

She said, "What I gathered from Blythe was that the book says that if we're truly mated, then your powers should've disappeared for three days. The powers that were allotted to me will remain, but we'll both share the ones you got from Mace." She shrugged. "You'll be able to hear mind speak with me, as well as Mace, and when we first mate, then our life forces will become one, and a tattoo will appear somewhere on our bodies." She brought her hand up to her neck.

"We haven't," she cleared her throat. "We haven't done it, so why do I have this?"

I smiled at her use of 'done it' and tried to keep the smile from overtaking my face.

"By 'done it' you mean have sex?" I teased.

She glared at me.

Grinning, I explained my theory. "My theory is just that, a theory, okay?" At her nod, I continued, "I think that, since we spent so much time together, that when you were in danger, our mating was changed. For Blythe and Keifer, they had to mate to solidify their bond."

She nodded, and then moved her hand in a continuous motion.

"For Nikolai and Brooklyn, their bond was forged by danger. If whatever bond we have with each other senses danger, then I believe that fate takes the reins in its hands and forces us together to keep each other safe. In your case, when I was around you and you encountered the dead chick, whatever bond we had solidified and forced our hand, so to speak," I expounded.

She licked her lips, then nodded. "And the tattoos?"

I grinned at that.

"I don't know," I admitted. "The others are all tribal in design. Ours is…not."

She snorted. "That, I can tell. Do you know how many people will look at you like you're an abusive asshole?"

I shrugged. "I'm sure they'll get over it."

She rolled her eyes.

"Let's go," she growled. "I'm hungry, and you have dragon work to do."

Twenty minutes later, when we arrived at the house, Wink turned to me and stared at me oddly, her eyes fixated on my neck.

"What?" I asked.

"I'm kind of glad," she whispered.

"Glad about what?"

"Glad that ours are different than theirs."

With that she left to run up the stairs, leaving me in a state of arousal that I wasn't sure Mace would much appreciate having pressed against his back.

Meaning, I was thirty minutes late, pissing off Jean Luc in the process.

"You're late, *mon ami*," Jean Luc growled.

"*Embrasse moi tchew,*" I growled.

Jean Luc laughed and flipped me off before he disappeared into the night.

I smiled as I remembered the first time I'd said that to Jean Luc.

Embrasse moi tchew meant 'kiss my ass' in Cajun French, and I'd gone out of my way to ask an old lady at a New Orleans style restaurant phrases and exactly how to pronounce them in order to say them to Jean Luc and surprise him.

He thought I was simple.

I wasn't. I just didn't want to talk.

Nobody could understand that I preferred to spend my time alone.

Well, I used to.

Now I kind of wanted to spend my time with a certain strawberry blonde haired wild child who kept me on my toes.

I'd admired her from afar for far too long. Getting to speak to her now, instead of watching her, was huge to me. I didn't want to spend my entire night on watch. I wanted to spend it in my bed…with her.

The entire shift I was patrolling I was in a bad mood, and an hour and a half before dawn, when Derek finally showed up for his shift, I was so beyond a good mood that it was almost comical.

"Finally," I muttered, walking away before I could give Derek a chance to settle.

Derek's annoyed curse had me wanting to laugh, but I was too fucking tired to be indulgent.

Everything ached, too.

Mace, for once, didn't fly me out of the way to get to my house. He flew me straight there, and I couldn't help but say 'thank you' the moment I dropped off his side.

You're welcome.

The moment I hit my front stoop, I unlocked the door with the keypad, punched in the code to halt the alarm, and closed and relocked the door.

Once I was inside, I rearmed the alarm, and quickly walked to the kitchen to down a glass of water.

I was careful to be as quiet as I possibly could, unwilling to wake up Wink if it wasn't absolutely necessary.

I got into my room and was stripping out of my clothes when I realized being quiet had been all for naught when I saw Wink sitting up in bed, reading.

"You're reading?" I asked. "Do you realize it's nearly five in the morning?"

She nodded.

"I found a good book to read," she admitted as she clicked a button on the side of her electronic device and set it on top of my nightstand. "Why are you so late?"

"Derek decided he wanted to show up an hour late," I muttered, starting on my pants.

Wink watched me undress without a word, even going as far as to pull the covers back to allow me entrance.

The minute my pants dropped, she gasped, and I smiled.

"By the way," I said as I slid in beside her. "I didn't wear underwear."

CHAPTER 9

Surprise sex is the best thing to wake up to…unless you're in prison.
-Fact of Life

Wink

By the time six o'clock rolled around, I gave up trying to sleep.

How I ever thought I'd be able to with a naked man in the same bed as the one I was in was beyond me.

I rolled to my stomach and lifted up onto my elbows, my eyes taking in all that was Ian.

He was a fitful sleeper, and by fitful, I mean terrible.

His arms and legs were everywhere, and I'd never seen someone sleep so restlessly.

I thought I was bad with my legs moving.

Ian was by far the worst. He slept like he was awake. Constantly, he'd move, twitch, strike out, and sometimes even speak.

His words at first hadn't made much sense, but after listening to him for the last two hours, I'd decided that Ian needed to talk to someone. Maybe multiple someones.

His first incoherent words were about a person named Mattie.

Mattie was apparently in danger somehow, but I'd yet to figure out how.

I'd gained over the last hour that Mattie was Ian's long lost sister. She was his exact opposite in complexion, and she had a dog named Judy.

Judy had died right along with their parents.

That last part I'd gathered through some fucked up connection that Ian and I had.

At first I hadn't realized what I was doing, but it didn't take long to figure out I was reading him, somehow, by my hand placed on his.

His words and meanings had become clearer the moment I'd placed his hand into mine, and had stayed clear until I'd dropped his hand twenty minutes ago.

In the last twenty minutes, he was as restful as I'd ever seen him.

And it was eerie since the last two had been anything but.

I'd gone back to reading my book I'd put down when he came in and had done a fantastic job at ignoring the world around me.

Until that last twenty pages I'd read that depicted the most realistic sex scene I'd ever read in my life.

Now I was hot, horny, and lying next to the world's sexiest man.

A man who'd kicked off the covers and was lying, in all his naked glory, right next to me.

I'd at first been reclining against the headboard, but had quickly changed positions when I realized how easy it was to see Ian's cock.

When I'd changed positions, I'd laid on my belly and had propped my Kindle up against the headboard, but quickly halted when Ian's big, huge, sexy body rolled over and pinned me to the bed.

Now I'd been lying in exactly the same spot for way too long, and I had what amounted to a proverbial flood in between my thighs.

With nothing else to do, I read, and continued reading until I hit about halfway through the first sex scene of the book.

I'd stopped because Ian's cock had started to rise.

The moment I'd shifted, he'd rolled, exposing that long, thick member to my curious eyes.

And I'd died.

Or, at least, it felt like I had.

I'd been with three men in my life, and none of them had a cock like Ian's.

Ian's would make a porn star proud, and it was a cock that should be molded so that tens of thousands of dildos could be produced in its likeness to memorialize its magnificence.

Yes, it was that good.

Slightly more tan than the rest of him, his cock was long—nearly nine inches or more if my guess was correct—and as thick as my wrist.

Granted, my wrist was on the daintier side, but the man's cock was anything but dainty.

He wasn't Coke can thick, but I'd definitely say it was beer bottle thick.

That thing would be a brute getting inside of me, especially since I'd never experienced anything quite like Ian's cock.

The purple tinted mushroom head of his cock was pulsing, and the veins that ran along the large...

"Are you going to stop staring one of these days and actually do something about what you're feeling?" Ian asked, amusement tinging his words.

My eyes shifted over to his face, and I blushed profusely as I realized he was awake and watching me.

"It's like a train wreck," I breathed.

"What makes you compare my dick to a train wreck?" he questioned, leaning up slightly onto his elbows.

I licked my lips involuntarily and replied with, "Because I can't help but look at it. Just like when you pass a train wreck. You can't help but look despite knowing that you shouldn't."

"What makes you say you shouldn't be looking?" he persisted.

I cleared my throat and leaned forward, scooting until our thighs touched.

"It's a bad idea to make this even more complicated than it already is," I said, my hand reaching forward.

He leaned forward as well, and soon I found myself with a handful of Ian's cock.

His hot…soft…silky… pulsing …cock.

I licked my lips again, and out of the corner of my eye I saw Ian's eyes become hooded.

"Fucking is not going to make this any more complicated," Ian said, his voice rough with something I couldn't place quite yet. "In fact, it might very well uncomplicate this."

I leaned forward, and suddenly found myself on my knees, my mouth only inches from the tip of him.

My eyes found his, and I just…gave up.

Stretching my tongue out, I licked the small drop of pre-come that beaded at the top, wondering idly whether it would taste good.

I'd had bad experiences with the taste of come, and to my pleasant surprise, Ian tasted scrumptious.

I swallowed his cockhead whole, and closed my eyes as a moan slipped out of my throat.

Ian's large cock trapped the moan before it could become audible; Ian felt it rather than heard it.

Which was all that mattered.

His hands came up to my head, sifted through my hair for the barest of seconds, and then disappeared to the bed where he clutched the covers on either sides of his hips.

I laughed at the amount of control he was able to hold on to.

Smiling inwardly, I started to lick his cock like a melting ice cream cone.

One lick up one side, curve around the top, and back down the other.

Round and round I went, sucking, licking, and tasting all that was Ian.

Before long, his hands were fisted so hard that I could hear his knuckles cracking with each downward lick.

"Take me into your mouth!" he demanded hoarsely.

I hummed in approval, and finally took him fully down my throat. So fucking deep that my throat felt like it was stretched to its limits.

"Ah, God," he groaned. "Fuck."

I pulled my mouth off of him and sat up to my knees.

The moment I was free of him, he pounced, hitting me bodily and throwing me back onto the bed.

"Lay there. Stay still."

I did as asked, not because I wanted to, but because he made me.

One hand flat on my chest to keep me down, he threw up the nightgown I'd slipped into before bed, and with one hard, quick wrench, tore my panties off my legs.

The loud *riiiiip* had me gasping in surprise as my entire body was jolted from the move.

My unbound breasts jiggled beneath my nightgown, and my entire body was pulled down the bed multiple inches with the force of his movement.

The moment I was bare to his gaze, he bent down and took one long inhale of my nether regions before he started to feast.

At first, he started out slow.

Tiny, gentle licks all around my clit at first before he'd relent and suck it into his mouth only to go back to teasing me with his tongue.

"Oh, sweet baby Jesus," I breathed, my hands going to his hair.

"Nuh-uh," he ordered. "No hands. Just me and your pussy."

I couldn't argue with that. Partly because he was giving me the best cunnilingus of my life. I'd never experienced better.

The other reason I couldn't argue was due to the fact that the second his finger breached my entrance, I lost my ability to breathe, and with it, speak.

I'd just decided that I couldn't hold it back any longer, and was on the verge of telling him to get up and fuck me, when he seemed to read my mind and his mouth left my pussy.

His large cock met the apex of my thighs, and he ground his hips down into me.

The moment my body met his, my mind started to run away with itself. Should we do this? What would happen if we did, and he changed? What if he thought that by having me once he owned me?

"Sure you're ready for what this is going to do to us?" he asked, reading my second thoughts.

I licked my lips, my eyes studying the seriousness in his eyes, and I nodded.

"Ready. So freakin' ready it's not even funny," I moaned, pressing my hips up to urge him inside.

He took the hint and withdrew his hips, letting his cock drag along the lips of my sex until the head rested against the entrance to my pussy.

And with infinite slowness, he parted my lips with that massive beast, and slowly sank inside until he could go no further.

I looked down and saw that not all of his cock was inside of me, and my bugged-out eyes shot up to his.

"We'll get there," he said, reading my thoughts or maybe just my expression. I didn't know. All I knew was that he was inside—mostly—of me, and it felt like heaven when he suddenly flipped to his back taking me with him.

"Ride me," he ordered as I continued to clench and unclench around him, trying in vain to make myself get used to the invasion.

"I don't think I can," I whispered, raising up a fraction and sinking back down on him.

Over and over again, I lifted up a bit more and then sank back down on him.

I did that for maybe a minute or two before Ian lost patience with my lack of movement, and then roughly took hold of my hips.

All of his patience disintegrated, and he yanked me down so hard that I was forced to take him all.

Every. Single. Delicious. Inch.

One second an orgasm unlike any I'd had before was building, and the next I was exploding in a blissful climax that rocked me to the core.

It slammed into me so hard—almost as hard as Ian's cock—that I lost all remaining breath in my body.

He quickly flipped us over, my back pressing into the mattress as my knees pulled up reflexively to push myself away from such unbelievable pleasure. But just like with everything else, he made me feel and didn't let me retreat.

He took my legs and placed them against his chest, my feet up by his ears, as he continued to pound into me.

Then, with his ungodly amount of strength, he lifted and pushed me down onto his length, filling me so full of him that my orgasm turned into something otherworldly.

I bit my lip to hold back my scream, but the move was in vain.

Most assuredly.

The backs of my legs hitting his belly and chest made a sharp smacking sound, spurring him on. Spurring *me* on.

"Jesus Christ," Ian hissed, the veins in his neck standing out as he pushed us both harder, farther into the depths of this hereto unknown pleasure.

He was so deep inside of me that I couldn't tell whether I was feeling pleasure or pain, but at that moment in time I wasn't sure that I cared.

Tomorrow, maybe I'd care.

But right now…well, right now I was so high on all that was Ian that I didn't think anything would matter tomorrow.

Only the now mattered.

The way he was making me feel.

The way I was making him feel.

I could feel exactly what I was doing to him, too.

The more I concentrated on him, the more I realized that we were feeding off each other.

He was getting harder by knowing the feel of him inside of me was getting me off.

I was getting slicker, allowing more than I ever would've allowed any other man to take, and that was all because of that connection.

My head started to lull as another orgasm started to rise through me.

My spine started to tingle, and my breath caught in my lungs.

Ian's body stiffened over mine, and I tried to pull my legs back to gain the momentum I needed to push myself over the edge.

I shouldn't have bothered.

Ian knew exactly what I needed.

Pinned beneath him, surrounded by him, his hips powered into mine.

His cock so hard and thick filled me up so well that I didn't want him to ever leave.

"Oh, my God," I breathed. "Please."

Ian's eyes, so fucking perfect I could barely stand to look at them, held mine.

And we both fell.

Something happened then. Something so profound that I knew I would never be the same.

Every single thing that had ever happened to me, that I'd ever participated in or felt was given to him in that moment.

And I received the same from him in return.

His hopes. His dreams. His desires. His everything. I now knew everything.

Our eyes locked, our gazes held, and we fell. Hopelessly, irrevocably and madly.

He knew everything there was to know, and he smiled.

"I was your first in a long time!" I whispered once we both came down.

He blinked, then grinned.

"You're so smooth! How the hell does that even work? I was a nervous wreck, and you're like an iron statue. Hells bells, Ian!" I exclaimed.

He was so sure of himself, so confident. Everything that I wasn't.

"I was waiting for you," he said, dropping his face down so he could place a small kiss on the corner of my mouth before he pulled away from me.

Horror flooded through me as I realized we didn't use a condom.

"We didn't use a condom!" I cried. "Oh, my God."

"I'm fixed," he muttered. "No worries there."

My brows furrowed.

"You're fixed?" I asked.

He nodded.

"Why?" I asked. "Why on Earth would you get 'fixed?'"

He looked at me like I wasn't seeing the whole picture.

"Search for it," he muttered.

Then he left, leaving me there to wonder what in the hell I'd just said to garner that kind of reaction from him.

Surely he didn't really think that he was unworthy like I was reading from him.

Surely.

Right?

Wrong.

That was exactly what he believed, very strongly in fact, and it was something that I realized much too late.

CHAPTER 10

If I had a Taser, I'd probably get curious and Taser myself...and that's why I don't have a taser.
-Fact of Life

Wink

I walked out of the bedroom eight hours later, searching for Ian for the tenth time that day.

I didn't know what I expected.

I'd gone through every room in his four-bedroom mini-mansion and hadn't found him yet.

Then I'd gone outside, played with a trio of blue dragons—dragons that Ian assured me weren't normally there, and it had to have been because they had come to see me—with really disconcerting eyes, and then I'd gone back inside. After sitting on my ass watching *Seinfeld* re-runs for over two hours, I'd finally gotten up to clean.

When I was done cleaning, I'd picked up my camera, which had magically appeared the other day in one of the spare bedrooms, along with all my other belongings, and walked outside to explore.

After taking a few hundred photos, I started to make my way back into Ian's house only to stop when I saw Keifer and Ian in the woods just beyond Ian's backyard.

I raised my camera and started taking photos of the two of them, knowing damn well and good that Ian knew I was there.

My focus, at first, had been the two of them, but then my camera lens took on a life of its own and focused in on Ian.

His eyes. The part of his lips. The slant of his eyes. The silver that streaked through his hair. His tattoo.

The same one that was on my neck.

Although his tattoo was more dainty in appearance. More like my hand than the one on my neck that looked like his.

Once I'd taken so many pictures that I knew I would have a hard time sorting through them all, I finally broke cover and walked out into the open.

Keifer saw me immediately and his eyes did something funny.

They filled with sorrow.

"Wink," Keifer said in a deeply grating voice. "I would like to apologize."

"For what?" I asked him absently as I made my way to Ian's side.

Ian stiffened when I wrapped my arms around his. Clearly, he wasn't over whatever the hell he'd gotten stuck up his ass today. It was obvious that I had my work cut out for me when Keifer left.

I smoothed my hand up Ian's strong arm, my fingers splaying against the soft skin of his inner arm.

"…for whatever harm I caused you after hitting Ian. It was never my intention to harm you in any way," Keifer was explaining.

My eyes moved from Ian's arm to Keifer's face.

"You meant Ian harm," I said.

Keifer winced.

"I'd received bad news," he explained.

I raised my eyebrow at him. "And that gives you the right to hit him because you didn't like what he had to say?"

Keifer scowled.

"He said my son isn't my son," Keifer growled, upset all over again.

"No," Ian interrupted. "If you'd have let me finish, I would've told you that your son wasn't your son when he's in that state where he's giving that vacant stare to you like he was doing when I walked into the room."

Keifer's eyes crinkled at the edges.

"What are you talking about?" Confusion was written all over Keifer's face, but I couldn't say I blamed him for feeling that way.

I was confused as well.

Ian took pity on us and gestured for us to follow him into the house.

I went without thinking about it, taking Ian's hand like it was the most normal thing in the world to do.

Keifer, however, stayed well back, keeping as much distance as possible between us without actually following so far behind that it became rude.

The moment we entered the kitchen, I walked to the coffee pot.

Ian had one of those old-time ones that you actually had to use a filter with coffee grounds.

Without much thinking about it, I made coffee like I did it every day, wondering if that would be my new normal.

I had missed two of my appointments in the last two days, and I'd miss one tonight as well, unless I could convince Ian to take me to it.

Something I hadn't thought he'd go for, so I didn't bother to ask.

"What?" Ian asked, sounding annoyed at something.

I turned to see Keifer staring around him in awe.

"I've never been inside here before," Keifer said. "It's nice."

Ian hummed, but otherwise didn't comment.

"You haven't asked to come over," I guessed. "Otherwise he would've allowed you entrance."

Keifer's lips pursed, and I turned back to the coffee, watching as it filled the last few drops.

"Let me see your phone," Ian ordered.

I turned to see Keifer handing him his phone, and I reached to the drying rack next to the sink and snagged three coffee cups, placing each on the counter in front of the coffee pot before filling each up three quarters of the way.

I filled mine and Ian's up, fixing it with milk and two sugars like we both liked.

Keifer's I left plain, setting the ceramic mug in front of him.

He nodded his thanks, and I moved to Ian, placing his at his elbow and leaning over his shoulder to look at what he was doing.

Pictures.

He was looking at pictures.

He was flipping through them so fast at first I was wondering if he was even looking at them. Then he got to one of a baby, one of the twins, and stopped. He flipped back to the one before it, switched back to the previous, and did it a few more times with the pictures before it before setting the phone down on the counter.

"Look at these two pictures," Ian instructed.

Keifer leaned over, pushing his coffee up so he could get closer, and studied the two pictures.

"What's wrong with it?" he questioned.

"Look at his eyes. The left one in particular."

"There's a light," I said, studying it right along with Keifer. "There's a light in one, and there's not one in the second picture, right?"

Ian nodded.

"That's right."

"What are you saying?" Keifer asked. "Is he possessed or something?"

"No," Ian said, shaking his head. "He's gone. In the first picture, the one with the light behind his eye, he's there. His soul is there." He flipped to the next photo. "In this one, his soul is gone."

"Where'd he go?" Keifer asked, his voice rising with worry.

"Your daughter can dream walk," Ian sat back in his chair. "Your son doesn't need his dreams. He can walk whenever he wants and he's aware and cognizant when he's doing it."

Keifer blinked right along with me.

"Should a baby as young as these children have such special powers?" I asked no one in particular.

Keifer and Ian shook their heads simultaneously.

"No," Ian answered. "Girls don't have any powers unless mated to a dragon rider. For Grace to have them, that's unusual in and of itself. Dragon riders normally get their powers around eighteen to twenty-one years of age. For Reed to already be experiencing powers as potently as he is, it means that he could be the most dominant dragon rider in the world."

"And the one and only thing people will kill to have in their employ," Keifer said, his eyes far away and haunted.

"Nobody's going to get Reed, Keifer," Ian promised. "Not just me, but the entire fucking dragon rider army will make sure of it. They'd have to get through not just you, but me, your mate. Nikolai, his mate. It'd be a bloodbath, and not one anyone could win, even Joseph."

"Who's Joseph?" I asked.

"Joseph was the man who killed my father and nearly killed Blythe and me when we first mated," Keifer explained, taking a seat on the barstool in front of the bar. His eyes were far away, and I knew that wherever he was at, it wasn't a good place to be.

"Do you want anything else to drink, Keifer?" I asked him.

Keifer's eyes snapped to me, and he shook his head.

"No, I'm not thirsty," he replied.

His stomach chose that time to growl its hunger, and I smiled.

"How about some eggs and bacon?"

He gave me a small smile, and I took that as my cue to feed him.

"How do you like your eggs, Keifer?" I asked.

"Over easy," he responded, his eyes going from me to Ian and back again.

Ian hid his grin and turned to the fridge, removing the eggs as well as a massive package of bacon.

"How much of this should I cook?" I asked him as he handed the package to me.

"All of it."

I blinked.

"What?" I asked.

"All of it," he repeated. "I want you to cook all of it."

"There's no way in hell y'all can eat all of this bacon," I informed him haughtily.

He grinned at me.

"Watch us."

Twenty minutes later, I realized that they could, indeed, eat sixty pieces of bacon between the two of them.

Holy fucking shit.

CHAPTER 11

Dear life, whatever motherfucker. Whatever.
-Ian

Ian

I arrived home after walking Keifer to the property line to find the kitchen clean. Clean for the second time that day.

Wink.

Bathroom, her beautiful voice rolled through my mind. *Will you bring me a washcloth?*

Wondering why in the hell she'd need a washcloth, I grabbed a stack of them out of the linen closet before heading her way.

I stopped to rid myself of my pants and shoes before stepping into the steamy hot room with only one thing on my mind.

Helping Wink wash her back.

However, the moment my eyes lit on Wink's body, submerged in my bathtub with bubbles covering most of her body, I froze.

Her breasts were playing peek-a-boo with the top of the water, and with every move she made, they would bob on top of the water, and my eyes couldn't help but be drawn to the movement.

"Bring it here," she ordered the moment she realized I was in the room with her.

I walked forward, not bothering to shield my raging hard on from her eyes, and stopped beside the tub.

"Here," I said, holding out the washcloth.

This close I could make out various body parts. A knee, the 'v' of her pussy.

Before I could take note of each and every body part I could see, she stood up and lifted her leg up on the lip of the tub.

"Get in," she ordered.

I blinked. "Why?"

She smiled at me, and then pointed at the water where she'd been sitting earlier.

Soap bubbles slid down her beautiful body, and I had to check the urge to grab her and force her to bend over the edge of the tub.

Instead, I questioned why I had bothered to wear underwear today. I pushed my briefs down my legs, and let them drop to my feet.

My cock bounced free of its confines, smacking against my belly, as Wink's eyes automatically went to it.

She licked her lips and I nearly groaned.

Hold it together, I said to myself.

"Why would you need to do a thing like that?" Wink asked, sugary sweet.

I grimaced, forgetting for a minute or two that she could hear my thoughts now if she desired to.

Placing one foot into the water, I hissed and pulled it back, water slinging everywhere.

"What?" she asked worriedly.

"Goddamn that's hot as fuck," I said, reaching my hand into the water to see if it really was as hot as my foot told me it was.

And I realized that my foot hadn't been mistaken. It was hot.

Hotter than hell.

"Why do you have it so hot?" I asked her, trying to sink my foot inside again.

"This is just how hot I like it," she replied. "Don't be a wiener. Get in."

I did, but by the time the water was up to my neck, I was nearly hyperventilating.

"I hope you never wanted kids," I teased through clenched teeth.

Her eyes filled with mirth.

"I want six," she informed me.

My mouth dropped open.

"You're shitting me, right?" I asked hopefully.

She shook her head. "No. I really do. I want six. Three boys and three girls."

My eyes were as wide as saucers, I was sure. "Why in the hell would you want that?"

She grinned. "It's a well-rounded number. I always wanted more siblings growing up, and I want my kids to have someone they can count on, always."

My heart literally melted, and my horror-stricken eyes slowly filled with understanding.

"I got a vasectomy when I was seventeen," I told her. "It was stupid, and I lied on my paperwork telling them I was twenty-one."

"Why?" she whispered, turning to face me, her back on the opposite wall of the tub.

"Because it seemed like the thing to do at the time," I replied, not having a good answer to offer her.

"That's sad." She looked at me with haunted eyes. "But, if your life was anything like mine, I could see why you'd want to do something like that."

I shrugged.

"It wasn't so bad once I was seventeen. When I was sixteen and younger, though…well, let's just say that life could've been better," I said, picking her foot up and bringing it over into my lap.

Wink's feet flexed, and her soft little toes grazed the top of my dick.

"I was nearly raped when I was four by my mother's boyfriend," Wink broke the silence.

My hand on her foot tightened nearly to the point of causing her pain, and she pulled the appendage away from me, sticking it back under the bubbles.

"When I was seven, I was taken away from my mother and placed in a state funded foster home," she continued. "When I was nine, I ran away from there because my foster father liked the money he got for taking in foster kids, but didn't like using that money to take care of them. My best friend, Shane, and I ran away and didn't come back. We lived on the streets until we were ten when we were caught by cops and returned to the foster system. This time, luckily, not to that same home."

When I stayed silent, she continued without needing to be prompted.

"It was the best thing that could have happened for me and Shane. We were placed in a home that was located about twenty miles outside of Dallas. There, we learned to ride horses, take care of ourselves and just be kids," she said the last part so softly that I almost didn't hear her.

"You sound like you got lucky there at the end," I observed.

Her eyes tilted up to me, and she smiled. "That's where I met my other best friend, Mattie."

I smiled.

I knew all of this. Not the running on the streets part for an entire year at the age of nine, but the fact that, from the age of ten on, she grew up in a foster home where she was loved and appreciated. What she didn't know, though, was that I've known of her for a very long time. Way longer than her employ with me.

"Mattie, Shane, and I were like three peas in a pod. We spent all of our waking hours together, and grew up to be very similar. Shane works with metal, just like me. Although, he's a lot better at it than I am." She smiled. "Mattie is a photographer, but where I specialize in portraits, she is a newspaper photographer. She works for the Dallas Times."

I knew that, too.

I knew everything there was to know about Wink.

I'd watched her sculpt her metal sculptures before we were an 'us.' For hours, I'd look through the small window of her studio and watch as sweat dripped down her chest, arms, and neck.

The sculptures that she'd created were beautiful, but they were nothing compared to the woman creating them.

Wink's eyes narrowed.

"You don't look surprised by any of this," she observed.

She was a smart cookie.

Even with me shielding my thoughts from hers, she knew when I wasn't being open with her.

"Mattie," I hesitated. "Mattie's my sister."

Her mouth dropped open.

"She's your what?" she asked, sitting up so fast that water sloshed over the tub's edge.

The outrage on her face was so comical that I nearly laughed.

Nearly.

Because the outrage was real.

For her friend and my sister, not for me.

"You're...you...You're," she sputtered. "You're an asshole!"

"What?" I asked, catching her before she could surge out of the bathtub and stomp away angrily. "Why?"

I found that I quite liked where she was, her breasts up high above the bubbles, on her knees, in front of me.

Her chest heaving wasn't a bad thing, either. Her nipples played peek-a-boo with the bubbles, going in and out, over and over again.

My cock, which had been cooperating until now, started to stiffen at the look of pure outrage on Wink's face.

I stifled a smile and reached for her, pulling her into my arms.

"Your sister thought you hated her," she whispered. "How am I supposed to choose between you?"

I smiled at her.

"You don't have to choose. I won't make you," I promised her.

"I will, unless you're willing to meet her," she replied. "I won't give her up unless you force me to."

"I'm not ready," I told her.

"It's been twenty years," Wink said gently. "You need to get over whatever bullshit you think you have going on, and put her out of her misery."

I let go of Wink, but she stayed in my arms and stared at me, her bright eyes boring into mine with such understanding now that it was unsettling.

When I tried to push her away she pulled her legs up and linked them around my waist, locking herself in place so I couldn't stand up and leave unless I took her with me or forcibly pushed her off. Something that I wouldn't do, and she knew it.

"I'm not a good person," I said. "I've never been a good person. The one and only good deed I ever did was make sure that she was okay. That she wouldn't suffer like I had."

She smiled at me sadly.

"Mattie knows that," she whispered, pressing her lips against mine. "She knows that you only want to protect her. Apparently, you made a lasting impression the last time she saw you."

"And what did I do?" I asked, hoping she didn't know.

"You killed the man who offered to help you raise her and then tried to force himself on her. Then you got her placed with someone who you trusted to ensure that whatever threat you perceived that was still out there couldn't touch her. Paid for her private school, and then for her college education. You send her money once a month, and still refuse to see her, even though the danger that was there is gone." Wink stroked my beard as she spoke, her eyes filled with barely contained pain. "Why do you do this to yourself and her?"

All my hopes were dashed when I realized that not only did she know most of it, she knew all of it.

"Because the threat that I've been hiding her from is still here. And now you're involved in it with me," I explained. "It's even more dangerous now than it has been."

"Blythe and Brooklyn told me that the threats to their lives were eliminated."

I shook my head.

"There's a whole organization of purists. We cut off the head, but it's the type of organization that, when you kill one, two more pop up in its place willing to do the job." I shook my head. "Seriously, that's why I stayed away from you as long as I did. This isn't a safe place. Not for the dragon riders; especially not for their mates."

"There hasn't been a damn thing that's happened in the time we've mated," she countered, angry now.

I pushed her off my lap during her moment of anger, and stood up.

My dick came to a stop directly in front of her mouth, but neither one of us took advantage of it, both of us too mad to consider that at the moment.

I stepped out onto the thick white mat and reached for a towel that hung on the back of the bathroom door while I spoke angrily.

"I don't really know how to tell you anything about what's going on," I said. "I can feel it, though. In my bones. So fucking deep that, sometimes it's like an ache that never goes away. Then shit like today happens, and I am sure."

"Shit like today?" she asked, standing now, too.

I nodded.

"Yeah," I said. "Dead carcasses left at the borders to our sanctuary."

"Why would you think that's bad?" she asked at my back. "Maybe it's just an accident. A product of nature."

I shook my head.

"No," I said. "They're testing us."

"What?" she asked as she followed me out into my room. "How?"

"When something's forced across the border, which is protected by Nikolai with a ward, then whatever it is that crossed dies," I explained.

Her eyes widened.

"I crossed that border!" she said. "And I'm fine."

I nodded. "Each of Keifer's men gave a blood oath to him the moment we swore fealty to him. That blood oath extends to our mates."

She breathed a sigh of relief.

"A little warning would've been nice," she muttered darkly.

I grabbed a pair of underwear from the top of my chest of drawers, only for them to be ripped from my hands the moment I raised my foot up to step into them.

Wink pushed me from behind, and I went to one knee in the bed, her weight taking me down.

She landed on my back, and I tried to buck her off me.

"Get off," I said harshly.

"No," she said, tightening her legs around my hips and sitting down until her bare pussy was sitting snug against my ass.

I sighed and decided to lay there, waiting to see what she'd do or say.

She didn't disappoint.

"I want you to say hello to your sister. She deserves it," she informed me haughtily.

I sighed.

"I'll see what I can do," I lied.

"We'll get there," she promised.

I snorted.

"No, we won't," I promised right back.

She dug her fingernails into my back, and I flinched.

"Get off me before I make you get off," I said through clenched teeth.

She snickered. "You wouldn't."

"Wouldn't I?" I challenged her.

She leaned forward and her breasts rubbed against my exposed shoulder blades, making my earlier erection stiffen once again.

Dammit.

Ruled by my cock.

"I touched the headboard a few minutes ago, while I was undressing for the bath," she purred into my ear. "You want to know what I saw when I did that?"

"What?" I asked her.

I knew what she saw.

It didn't take much to guess, anyway.

"You're not even going to try to guess?" she asked hopefully.

I shook my head.

"No," I muttered into the blankets.

She scored her nails down my back again, and a moan slipped from my lips.

"You're a very muscular man," she observed as she rubbed her hands up and down my back, her muscles stopping to knead certain muscles of my back before she moved on to the next ones.

I moaned into my comforter, the sound so tortured that the wench on my back laughed.

"Hush," I growled.

She ignored me and leaned forward, her lips right next to my ear.

"Your arms have muscles in them that I've never seen before," she whispered. "The next time you stroke your cock in this bed, I want to watch."

Lani Lynn Vale

CHAPTER 12

Smonday: The moment that a Sunday starts feeling like a Monday.
-Fact of Life

Ian

"You want to watch now?" I asked her. "'Cause I'm about to come whether you want me to or not."

She giggled.

"Oh, yeah. I want to watch you stroke that cock now," she whispered, desire practically dripping from her voice. "Do you know what I did in the bath while I waited for you to come back?"

I didn't need to know.

The moment my back hit the coolness of the tub, the scene had replayed in my mind, blasting into the forefront of my brain like it'd always been there.

"Fuck me," I said, rolling over and dislodging her from my body.

She laughed as her back hit the bed, but it quickly died when she saw the state my cock was in.

"Do it," she ordered.

I gritted my teeth and grasped my cock in one work-roughened fist.

Her eyes widened when I started to stroke the length of my cock, pulling in rough tugs that would've looked downright painful to anyone else.

Me, though? Well, I liked it rough.

The rougher the better.

Something she was just now realizing.

My other hand moved down to my balls, and I started to tug, gently at first until before long I was working them just like I was my cock.

My eyes had closed, but the moment I heard Wink moan, my eyes shot open.

I found her only inches away from my cock, her hot mouth so close that I should've felt the heat from her breath on the tip of my dick.

Her tongue shot out the moment our eyes made contact, and the hot tip of her tongue met the small drop of pre-come that was pebbled at the slit of my cock.

"Fuck," I hissed.

"You taste good," she whispered silkily.

"Take more into your mouth," I ordered.

She shook her head and went up to her knees, then started to shuffle down the bed to where my head was resting on two pillows.

She yanked them both out from under my head, and I fell flat on the bed next to her knees, my eyes fully taking in her state.

"You want me?" I asked her.

"I want your mouth."

"Where?" I persisted.

"On me." She widened her legs, letting me see the wetness between her legs.

It was so copious that it slickened her thighs.

"Come ride my beard then, baby." I continued to work my cock, slower now than I had been doing it before.

She smiled at me timidly, her bravado fading.

"Now," I ordered. "Use my beard like your own personal saddle."

Her eyes widened, and I winked.

"Come on, I don't bite."

She slowly moved until she straddled my face between her thighs, her knees digging into the bed by my ears.

Her pussy hovered over my face, inches away.

I didn't move, though, instead letting her come to me.

And come to me she did.

One second her pussy was too far away for me to reach, even with my stiffened tongue, and the next she was practically smothering me with her cunt.

"Fuck," I muttered, but the syllable was lost in the lips of her sex.

Tongue darting out, I started to lick her clean, dipping it in and out of her sex to taste her like a fine wine.

My nose hit her clit, and her back bowed off the bed like I'd struck her with a live wire.

"Oh, God," she whispered frantically. "I've been holding off for you."

I knew that, too.

I'd watched her bring herself to the brink of orgasming not once, not twice, but four times.

"Give me your fingers," she pleaded.

I set one single digit at her entrance and circled the opening as my mouth found its way back to her clit.

Her hands latched onto my beard of all things, and then she tugged forward, and my entire face was covered by her pussy.

"I need more," she said urgently, jackknifing away and rolling over until she presented me with her backside. "Fuck me."

"Where did my sweet little Wink go?" I asked her, crawling up between her legs.

The rough palms of my hands slid up the backs of her thighs to her backside.

The minute my hands encountered the skin she pushed back, urging me on silently.

"Still," I said, punctuating that announcement with a slap to her backside.

She gasped, and it wasn't pain that flared up through our mating bond, but excitement.

"Oh darn," she whispered brokenly. "I'm going to fucking hell."

I laughed at her succulent words. "There's going to be fucking, but I doubt hell will be involved unless too many orgasms is your version of hell."

She glared at me over her shoulder.

"Are you going to do anything about this?" She pushed her ass backwards. "Or are you going to talk and play all day?"

My hand tightened on her ass cheek.

"What is it that you're wanting here, Wink?" I asked. "Fast and hard? Slow and soft? Use your words."

"You damn well know exactly what I want," she said. "I want you to fuck me. If I wanted slow and sweet, I would've found some other man. I know you don't do slow and sweet."

"You don't think I could do slow?" I asked, walking up on my knees until my cock kissed her entrance.

"I have no doubt that you can do slow," she said. "What I have doubts about is the 'sweet' part."

"Why's that?" I wondered, fisting my cock and dragging it up through the folds of her pussy.

She moaned into the bedspread, but managed to twist her head to the side once she was done to say, "You don't have a sweet bone in your body. Not when it comes to this, anyway. Now get on with it, or I'll take care of myself."

I chuckled and started to sink my cock inside of her, filling her so slowly that she started to curse.

"See what I mean about the 'sweet' thing?" she moaned. "If you were being sweet, then you'd give it to me like you knew I wanted it."

That was true. I knew exactly how she wanted it, down to the very last thrust of my hips.

She wasn't ready for that kind of fucking. Yet.

She needed to be warmed up and primed before she could take it that rough.

"Why do you think I played with myself while I was in the tub?" She pushed backwards, meeting my hips in a rough thrust that forced the headboard into the wall.

Taking that as a sign, I pulled out nearly all the way, letting the tip of my cock caress her entrance before I slammed back inside.

My hands tightened on Wink's hips to hold her in place so my exuberance didn't knock her off the bed, and she nearly collapsed completely to her belly the moment I filled her for a second time.

"Jesus," she yelped. "Harder!"

I gave it to her harder, not giving it all I had until she was ready.

Just when I'd started to find a rhythm as I filled her with my cock, Wink stopped what she was doing and crawled out from under me, causing me to freeze at the abruptness of the movement.

"Lay down," she ordered, pointing to the bed beside my knees.

Looking down at my raging cock that'd been inside of her only moments before, I decided to do what she asked and lay down.

The moment I did she moved to straddle my hips, and I watched as she did.

She took my length in her hands, and positioned it at her portal.

"Ready?" she asked, hovering just above the tip.

I nodded my head and gritted my teeth as I did.

"I'll go slow so I won't hurt you," she teased.

My eyes nearly crossed when she took me back inside—none too gently might I add.

"Fuck me," she breathed.

I started to move in and out, but there wasn't much I could do without taking control of her and the situation, and it was clear in my mind that she wouldn't appreciate it. Not yet, anyway.

"Oh, God," I growled, eyes getting heavy. "Ride me, Mama."

"Mama?" she asked, sounding amused.

I growled at her.

"Mama," I agreed.

"I kind of like it," she whispered. "Can I call you Daddy?"

I huffed out a laugh. "You can call me whatever the fuck you want to call me as long as you fucking ride me!"

She snickered as she lifted up to her full height at knee level, then slammed back down, taking me so deep inside that my breath stalled in my chest.

"God," she breathed. "You feel so good inside of me."

I could do nothing but nod as my hands went up to her breasts, my fingers tugging and sliding over her nipples so I wouldn't take over control like I really wanted to do.

She gasped and leaned into my hands, then surprised the shit out of me by leaning backwards.

Her hands went backwards to come to a rest on my shins just under my knees.

The new position put her whole body on display, as well as pulled her nipples away from my pinching fingers.

But there was her clit that was now peeking out from its hood between the lips of her sex for me to see.

Not to mention the sight of her pussy, stretched so full, and moving up and down the entire length of my cock.

"Stop," she whispered. "You're going to make me come too fast."

I looked up at her and grinned.

"You need to learn to turn it off," I told her, my eyes going back to continue watching her pussy working me. I moved my hands to her sex to spread her lips even wider, giving me a better view than before, which I would have thought was impossible.

"I don't want to turn it off," she said. "It's so much better this way. It's like I'm fucking you, and seeing it from my point of view, on top of seeing how it feels from your point of view. Maybe later, when you pee,

I can touch your back and experience that through you, too."

I huffed out a laugh, my eyes closing.

I never thought laughing during sex was a possibility, but damned if she didn't teach me something new every day.

Experiencing sex through her eyes might be something I would try later, but right now I was too overwhelmed by my own feelings to have hers inside of me, too.

Her pussy clenched when I thought about having my tongue inside of her at the same time I was taking her. Although physically impossible, the mere thought of it made her entire sheath clench so hard around my cock.

"Sometimes, I think you're such a choirboy," she informed me, moving her knees from beside my hips to plant her feet next to my hips. "But then you go and have thoughts like that one."

The new position spread her legs wider, and my already beautiful view turned into something so out of this world that the release I'd been holding off, by sheer force of will, slammed into me.

Unable to help myself, I started to come.

In fact, I came so hard that the roar that was forced out of my throat startled us both.

My body bucked, practically throwing Wink into the air in my exuberance.

I'd just closed my eyes in hopes of regaining my wits when there was a knock on the door.

Well, more of a pound rather than a knock.

"Wink!" the woman screamed, pounding harder now. "Oh, my God! Someone needs to call 911!"

Wink startled and stared at the door to the bedroom with unseeing eyes, causing me to nearly laugh at the cuteness of it all.

"You invite someone over without telling me?" I teased her.

Her bleary, tired eyes moved over to me, and then back to the door before she tossed the covers off.

"I know you're in there!" a woman yelled in indignation.

I looked over to Wink, brows drawn in confusion.

Nobody, and I do mean nobody, came up to my house. A, because my house wasn't easily accessible and there was a perimeter alarm on the property lines. It wasn't on right now, unfortunately. And B, because aside from the other dragon riders, the mailman, the UPS guy and Wink, nobody knew it was there.

"Holy shit," Wink breathed, rolling off of me and grabbing a pair of pants up off the floor. "So I might've forgot to tell you something. I gave someone your address. I invited her over to see that I was all right, and…" she trailed off as more pounding sounded at the door.

She was wearing my pants.

I also noticed how, when she stepped into the legs one by one, I could see that the inside of her thigh was slickened with my release.

Feeling somewhat excited at the sight of my come on her body, I followed behind her, nowhere near as fast as she had.

I actually stopped to clean myself, not worried that anything would happen to Wink.

Not only was Mace watching over the house, but so were Jean Luc and his dragon, Tele.

Rising voices rose from the living room as I heard the door shut, and then a whispered hiss of voices followed those high voices.

I washed my hands and found a pair of jeans off the hanger in the closet, shrugging them on without underwear before following the pants with a white t-shirt from the selection that hung on the opposite side of the closet.

Wink's doing.

I was just contemplating whether to put my socks and shoes on when I realized that I was stalling.

I didn't want to see who was on the other side of the door.

I knew who it was.

Knew the moment I heard her enter the house.

I'd have to have a talk with her about walking into unknown people's houses and wandering around without knowing what she was walking into.

My sister was within a stone's throw of me, and I was freaking out.

My palms were sweating, and I was close to hyperventilating.

I was also looking at the door like it was a snake about to strike.

With no other recourse, I ran.

Opening the window, I yelled for Mace in my mind, and he flew up from the shadows like he'd been shot.

The moment he was close enough, I launched myself from my bedroom window, which happened to be two stories up, and landed on Mace's back with a thump.

Mace either didn't notice the graceless move or didn't care, because he didn't comment at all, which he would've normally done.

However, my mood must've made itself known because he flew without me ordering him to, and we were high in the sky before he said his first word.

You're running.

Yes, I replied.

What's wrong?

"Why do you care?" I asked him acerbically.

Because, young master, I've always cared. It's easier for you to think that I don't care than for you to think that I do. I would've never gotten as far as I have, had you realized how much I truly do care about you.

I froze at those words.

"What are you talking about?" I asked, worry stiffening my spine.

If I'd been like Keifer, caring about you almost from the moment he realized you were a dragon rider, what would you think of me? Would it be the same as you thought of him? Keifer loves you. Jean Luc cares deeply. Everyone does. They're scared of you, but they'd be lost without you. You offer them quiet balance that they otherwise wouldn't have, and you're always there for each of them without having to be asked twice. Keifer knows your worth. Why do you think he tries to get you to move to the sanctuary so often?

I closed my eyes and thought about that. Thought about everything really, and I realized two things.

One, I was being a coward.

Two, I wasn't alone and never really had been. I'd isolated myself in my house, but I'd never actually been alone.

Jean Luc came over every day before his shift and shot the shit with me until our shifts started.

Derek asked my opinions on certain bills or laws that the government was enacting, trying to garner my opinion on them before they actually took effect.

Ford and Alaric, before they'd been sent to different sanctuaries to protect them, had come over every Monday night and watched Monday Night Football with me during football season.

Keifer came over every morning to hear reports, then to reiterate that he'd love for me to move into the sanctuary.

Then there was Nikolai extending the sanctuary's shield to protect my house.

Then there was Wink.

Although she hadn't known me as long as the other dragon riders, she knew me better than them all.

She wanted me to meet my sister, and she would know best, as one of my sister's best friends, then I was willing to meet her.

"Take me home" I ordered Mace.

Mace banked hard right, and then we were heading in the opposite direction.

CHAPTER 13

If you're ever in a fight with a woman, and she says, 'Wow' and then proceeds to adjust her ponytail, you should probably run.
-Fact of Life

Wink

"What are you talking about?" my best friend practically yelled. "Dragons? Are you fucking crazy?"

I smiled.

"Dragons," I said. "Let me have your hand."

I held my hand out for her to place hers in mine, and proving that she trusted me despite my crazy talk, she gave me her hand and waited patiently.

I grinned at Mattie and closed my eyes, opening the gift like Ian had mentioned to me earlier in the night.

To my amazement, the practice worked and everything that I ever needed to know about Mattie appeared in my brain like it'd been there all along.

"What did I tell you about eating all that chocolate cake," I opened my eyes and glared at my friend. "You know what it does to your stomach."

Mattie grimaced.

"I'm a stress eater," she said defensively. "You know that."

I grinned and let go of her hand.

"You've had two broken bones in your life. You ate fish and peas for lunch, a cheeseburger and onion rings for a snack around two, three pieces of chocolate cake for dinner, and five tacos from Taco Bell on your way here." I ticked off the things she'd eaten in the last six hours, and watched as Mattie's face contorted in amazement.

"You're not shitting me," she whispered. "Holy fucking shit! And your neck tattoo looks cool and all, but you won't be able to go out into general population with that on your neck. And there is still the mystery man that you haven't introduced me to yet. And, furthermore, you missed three appointments this week. I can't believe you did that. You know how important it is to establish one's portfolio. Not to mention they already left bad reviews on your website about how you pawned them off on your colleague at the last minute."

I grinned.

I *had* done that.

Although Mattie was a good photographer, she didn't like to do portrait work on actual people. Taking photos of actual people would require her to have to talk to them, and she didn't do that if she could help it.

Mattie was an introvert to the nth degree.

A person couldn't be any more introverted than she was.

"And I appreciate you taking them for me when you couldn't get a hold of me," I smiled.

"Why did I have to take them for you?" she persisted. "Why have you been missing for days without a word to me or Shane?"

I grinned.

"You're not going to believe me," I told her. "And I did call you. I gave you the address, didn't I?"

She gave me that look, the one that clearly said that she wasn't amused and that she resented the fact that she had to come looking for me after I'd left her a voicemail about where I was.

"I believed you about dragons and magic," she said. "Now tell me, or I'll call Shane and tell him where you are."

I rolled my eyes.

"Shane obviously wasn't worried about me if he's not here helping you beat down Ian's door," I muttered, not thinking what that name would do to her.

Mattie stiffened and her eyes went to the door in question.

"Ian?" she asked, her heart written all over her face.

Ian.

What she didn't know was that my Ian was *her* Ian.

She was about to have the shock of a lifetime, especially when I heard the door open and Ian step through.

"Ian," I confirmed.

Ian's eyes moved from me to his sister and stayed there.

"Well, where's this Ian of yours?" she asked, picking at invisible lint on her jeans. "I think I need a little more explanation than your man is a dragon rider and that his name is Ian. I think I would like a lot more, in fact."

I smiled at her.

"Ian?" I called.

Ian's head turned from Mattie to me, and then I saw him swallow visibly before taking a step in Mattie's direction.

With her back facing the door, she had no clue what was coming at her back.

I did, though, and what I saw on Ian's face was hauntingly beautiful.

"Mattie?" Ian's voice cracked. All the emotion he was feeling was clearly written all over his face, as well as dripping from his voice. Remorse. Love. Hope.

Mattie stiffened, and I saw the instant she realized that this wasn't a joke. That this was all real.

"He's real, isn't he?" she whispered. "You found him."

A statement, not a question.

She knew he was standing behind her.

The trembling started in her hands, moved right up her arms and straight to her lips, which started to wobble before the first sob tore free of her chest.

Ian moved in front of her, enveloping Mattie's hands with his before the first tear even made it to the bottom of her cheek.

"I always knew," she whispered, tears tracking down her face at a fast clip.

"Knew what?" Ian asked, just as shaken up as Mattie.

"That she would bring you to me."

CHAPTER 14

I have a get wussy.
-You read that wrong.

Ian

I left my house under the cover of night.

"You good?" Jean Luc asked.

I looked up, surprised to see him standing there.

"Will you do me a favor?" I asked him.

"Sure, *mon ami*," he said. "What do you need?"

He looked almost surprised that I asked, and it took everything in me not to smile.

"Will you go inside, keep my woman and my sister company?" I paused. "My sister…she's not in the right frame of mind; try to make sure she doesn't leave."

Jean Luc's mouth tipped up into a grin, his blazing white teeth standing out starkly against his tanned skin.

"I didn't know you had a sister," he grinned. "I'll love meeting her."

I rolled my eyes, but the anger that would've come not even a few weeks ago is now gone, and in its place is contemplation.

It wouldn't break my heart to have my sister with a man like Jean Luc.

However, what *would* break my heart would have my sister with someone like Farrow, the stupid motherfucker that was now walking up behind Jean Luc.

"Don't," I said, holding my hand up.

Jean Luc froze and turned, his movements sluggish and difficult, almost as if he were trying to move through quicksand.

"Stop it," I said once I realized that Farrow had been stupid enough to use his power—the one that allowed him to affect others by telekinesis. "He's going to fucking kill you when he gets himself loose."

Farrow grinned.

"Is that right?" he asked.

My eyes narrowed.

"What is your problem?" I asked. "Do you just like being a douche to everyone who gives a shit about you?"

Farrow lifted his lip in a silent snarl.

"I've been instructed by the high and mighty King of dragons himself to come over here and offer my services," he bowed slightly. "So here I am, to follow the Prince of awesomeness as he does his nightly routine."

I lifted my hand in a placating gesture to Jean Luc, but the moment he worked himself free, he was gone.

See, Jean Luc wasn't like the rest of us.

His powers weren't defensive. They were all offense.

That was why he was often overlooked—why people looked at him and didn't see a dangerous man.

Apparently, they hadn't pissed him off like Farrow did, though.

The moment he was able to move himself out of Farrow's hold, he moved like lightning, gathering himself up and then he was just gone.

Jean Luc can fly.

He could also…

A branch from the tree above Farrow fell, knocking him out before he even realized he should be paying attention.

Jean Luc's powers were of the knock-them-out-and-kill-them variety.

As I was saying, he could fly. He had superhuman strength. He could move things with his mind. And he could get himself free of any hold or lock—as he'd done with Farrow and his telekinetic ability.

It didn't help that Farrow was still so new to his powers. He didn't have the same control, nor had he participated in the fights that Keifer used to test our abilities.

"Jean Luc," I warned before the next branch came down. "He's a stupid kid."

Jean Luc dropped down, landing on the balls of his feet with one hand planted into the earth, and glared at the stupid pile of shit.

"I can't fucking stand him," he growled. "The kid is a fucking piece of crap who deserves to be quartered and cooked."

I snorted and turned toward the door.

Wink.

Wink's head appeared moments later in the parted drapes that covered the window of the front room of my house.

Come here.

My sister's head appeared next, first looking at me and then her eyes went huge at the sight of Jean Luc standing next to me.

I rolled my eyes at the whispered communication that went on between the two of them while they made their way outside.

"Yeah, Ian?" Wink asked as she stepped outside.

She had her hand around Mattie's wrist, hauling her with her as they breached the outside steps.

"Mattie," I said. "This is Jean Luc. Jean Luc, this is my sister Mattie."

Jean Luc nodded his head. *"Cherie."*

"Jean Luc is going to stay with you while I do patrol tonight," I said. "We're going to…"

I stopped when Mattie's phone rang.

She cursed and fumbled it out of her back pocket before placing it to her ear.

"Hello?" she answered.

Shock fell over her face, and then tears started to gather in her eyes.

"Okay," she said. "I'll be there as soon as I can."

She hung up and we waited for her to explain the call, me more so than anyone else.

"My house caught on fire tonight," she said when she realized we were waiting. "I have to run to my house and give them some information."

"Is it okay?" Wink asked as she looked at her best friend worriedly.

"They said it was a total loss. They weren't even able to get my neighbor out of his house before it spread to three other houses surrounding mine."

I swallowed as something, a wave of fear, washed over me.

"I'm coming with you." I took a step forward.

She held up her hand to stop me.

"No," she said. "You just told us you had to go to work, not even ten minutes ago. I'll be fine on my own."

I looked over to Jean Luc, who understood immediately.

"I'll go," he offered. "I'm done for the night. Is that acceptable?"

When she looked like she'd protest, Wink butted in.

"You don't know what they're going to need from you, and you don't even have a car. You're going to need to lean on someone for now," Wink said gently.

"I'll call Shane," Mattie suggested. "And I also have the Uber app, which is what I used to get here in the first place."

Wink barely hid her smile.

"Shane's working today," she said. "I just spoke with him an hour ago. He said he was going into his lair, and you know what happens when he goes into his lair."

"He doesn't take his phone so he can work without interruption," she growled in frustration.

I barely hid the smile that started to overtake my face.

She was uncomfortable at the thought of Jean Luc going with her.

That was just too bad. If she didn't want him, she'd get me.

Either way, someone would be taking her where she needed to go.

"Just give in," Wink snorted. "One of them is going to go with you."

Mattie grimaced and forced a smile. "Okay, Jean Luc, I hope you're ready for a wild, eventful night."

Jean Luc nodded his head. "I have a car at my place, but it's not anywhere close."

He looked at me, and I nodded at her.

"She knows."

Mattie's eyes widened.

"You're a dragon rider, too?"

Did her voice get higher in the last twenty seconds, or is that just me? I asked my woman silently.

Wink's lips tilted up in a smile.

She's excited. Leave her alone, Wink chastised me gently.

Ready, Freddy? Mace asked, touching down at my side.

I patted his neck and waved to my sister.

"Promise to call me if you need me," I ordered her.

The wide, excited eyes that met mine were freakin' beautiful.

"Holy shit," she breathed, getting her first good look at Mace.

I looked at him, too, and wondered for the first time if he realized just how gorgeous he was.

Mace was over sixteen feet in length and as wide as a train car. He was stocky and short, but he made up for that shortcoming (in his eyes, not mine) with his beautiful coloring.

Midnight blue with streaks of neon blue that ran all over his chest and back.

He had spikes midway down his back all the way to the tip of his tail, and bright blue eyes the color of lightening.

He had bright, white sparkly teeth—all the better to eat you with.

I know, I'm beautiful.

I rolled my eyes and mounted his back, climbing up until my knees were resting on either side of his neck.

"Call me the minute you know anything," I asked Jean Luc.

He nodded his head and whistled.

His dragon landed at his feet within twenty seconds of his call.

"Oh, holy shit," Mattie whispered.

Wink giggled and waved, blew me a kiss, and then disappeared back into the house.

I waited until my sister mounted Jean Luc's dragon, Tele, before taking off for my usual scheduled patrol.

My brother with you?

I looked over to find Keifer circling the grounds of my house, and I shook my head.

He's asleep.

Keifer's gaze darkened.

Why? he asked.

A grin split my face.

He tried to hold Jean Luc still while he had a discussion with me.

Keifer cursed and had his dragon circle around until he landed by his still-knocked-out brother.

Jean Luc waved at Keifer as he too took off, and I urged Mace to take a hard right.

Let's do our normal route, only backwards this time.

Mace pumped his wings, and suddenly we were high above the trees, and I felt like I could breathe easier. The feeling of riding on my paired dragon was exhilarating. Words couldn't explain how right it felt to be up high above the ground where the air temperature was cooler. Where people and buildings seemed insignificant. Where I could ride, and feel the wind in my hair, and not have to worry about someone hitting me with their car. It was quiet…so freakin' quiet.

It was an entirely freeing experience, and one that would only be better if Wink was up there with me.

I love you, but this bed is heavenly.

I sent a mental kiss to Wink, and then shut the door on our link. Not completely, though. I did it just enough that I knew what was going on with her, but she wasn't privy to my every thought and feeling.

The same went both ways, though.

This would be a time for Wink to reflect on her day without me sitting front and center in her brain, listening to every damn thing that went through her thoughts.

We flew for what felt like minutes, watching, calculating, and learning.

We passed markers in the land, examined property lines, as well as the shield boundaries that kept out any unwanted guests.

We checked on The Heart, felt the exhilaration at being so near, and then zipped through the night like we were one with the wind.

CHAPTER 15

I rode a dragon and I liked it.
-Wink's secret thoughts

Wink

Ten hours later

I rolled over in bed, my eyes going to the light shining through the window.

"Ian?" I called, rolling over to look at the bed beside me.

He appeared almost as if he'd sensed me waking, and I smiled at him.

"What time is it?" I asked him.

"Twenty minutes until one," he said, coming around to my side of the bed.

My eyes closed, and then snapped back open.

"Ian!" I yelled, scrambling out of bed. "You were supposed to wake me up two hours ago! I have a session in the park!"

His brows furrowed. "I thought you said that was tomorrow."

"It is," I grumbled. "Or was. I told you yesterday that it was tomorrow."

He shrugged. "I've been checking on my sister and the shop."

"What shop?" I questioned him as I searched for pants. "And how is she doing?"

"Her house is gone," he said. "As for my shop, it's my woodworking shop."

"You make wood?" I teased, looking over my shoulder at him as I pulled my pants up and over my hips.

His eyes were on my ass, though, and not on the question.

"I do," he confirmed. "I harvest my own trees and mill them into boards, logs, and beams."

My mouth dropped open.

"How did I not know that yet?" I asked. "We've been together for weeks now, and this is the first I've heard of it."

He shrugged.

"Been doing it since I was sixteen and working for an old man who used to own a mill," he explained. "I bought it from him about two years ago."

"Doesn't Keifer own a garage?" I asked, grabbing my shirt that I pulled out of the top of my pile.

"No," he smiled. "He owns a chain of them. Vassago Motors."

My mouth dropped open.

"You're shitting me," I said in surprise. "They're fucking everywhere!"

He nodded in agreement as he lifted the shades of the window. "They are, which is how and why Keifer's able to afford a great big place like this."

He pointed out the window, and I squinted, just barely able to see the tops of the sanctuary.

"Are you coming with me?" I asked him.

He gave me a look that quite clearly said what he thought of that absurd question.

"You can't wear that, though," I told him, pointing at his shirt, that I just now realized was covered in sawdust.

He looked down at the shirt that said, 'Drink Up, Fuckers.'

"Why not?" He pinched the shirt and pulled before letting it go, causing a cloud of sawdust to fall off his shirt and land in an arc all around him.

I gritted my teeth and vowed to make him vacuum later before heading to the closet for my shoes.

I was pleasantly surprised to find not just the one pair of shoes I'd been going for, but all of my clothes that'd been in my closet at my apartment.

Somewhat excited that he'd brought my belongings, I picked out a comfy pair of pants and an old t-shirt, as well as my old Nikes that looked like they'd seen better days.

I'd be doing a shitload of walking, and likely running around after the couple's children and dog, so I didn't want to be stuck in ones that hurt my feet.

I didn't bother to do much more than brush my teeth and use the restroom before I was dragging Ian out the door.

"Where are we going?" he asked.

"To my apartment," I said. "I need to get my other camera and the rest of my lenses and equipment."

He cleared his throat. "Your stuff's here."

I stopped.

"What?" I asked.

"I had it brought here, along with the rest of your shit."

"Where?" I asked, looking around his house.

He pointed to the door that led to the backyard, and I followed his directions to a shed I'd only seen, but not been into.

"But…why?" I asked.

He gave me another one of those 'are you kidding me' looks, and I stifled the urge to smile.

"Your apartment was broken into three times by your neighbor before I decided to bring all your belongings here," he said. "I was able to recover your panties and computer, as well as your camera, but I chose to throw the panties away, and store the rest until you asked about them."

I grinned at him and twisted the knob to the shed, freezing the moment I got inside and saw what he'd done.

It smelled like fresh cut wood, sweet and clean, and I loved it instantly.

The walls were made of cedar planks, and the floors were much the same.

At just a little bit over ten by ten, the entire thing was just about perfect in size.

"This is like an office," I said in awe. "Is this yours?"

He nodded his head. "It was. Then I moved to my new shop and didn't have use for this place anymore. I used to do some woodworking in here, that's what you smell."

"It's nice," I told him honestly. "What are you going to do with it now?"

"Now…" he turned his eyes to study me. "It's yours. If you want it, that is."

I was already nodding my head.

"Oh, I want it."

He pulled a set of keys out of his pocket.

"I just unlocked it this morning, but usually it's locked. Here are the keys." He gave them to me, dropping them into my outstretched hand and smiling as he did.

"Where's my camera stuff?" I asked him, looking back down at my watch.

"Check the shelves over there," he gestured to the wall to ceiling shelving unit that was all the way across the room. "I didn't see them unpack it, but I know it's here because Jean Luc asked me where he thought that I should put it."

I found it with a loud '*ah ha!*' and came running toward him.

"Are we taking the dragon or your car?" I asked.

He grinned at me.

"Neither."

Thirty minutes after we pulled up into the park that I was shooting at, and I couldn't have been more elated.

That was my first official long ride on Ian's Harley.

Ian, apparently, used to ride his bike quite a bit before I came into the picture.

Now, though, he had too much on his hands.

That, or it was raining, which seemed to be the norm in our state at the moment.

Today, though, was an absolutely beautiful day, and couldn't be better for the pictures I was taking of the soon-to-be-newlyweds and their about-to-be-blended family.

I spotted them the moment we pulled in, and I dismounted and started waving almost immediately.

"Hello!" I called as I made my way toward them, slinging my bag over my shoulder.

The bride to be waved at me and started forward.

The moment she stepped in my direction, though, the man behind her grabbed her arm and pulled her back.

He held up his phone, and then gave her an apologetic look before he answered it and walked off.

I waited for her to make her way to me, and then smiled at her.

She grimaced back.

"I sure do hope he remembers we're getting married in a week. He better not get himself tangled up in work."

I laughed.

"I'm sure that's not on the top of his list of priorities at this point," I replied. "Are you ready?"

At least I hoped not.

"Do you want to go ahead and start with the kids?" she asked. "My kids, and Leyland's, are over there. We can just do us at first, and work him in once he gets past whatever it is that's making him yell."

I agreed, but surreptitiously tossed a look over my shoulder to where Ian had stopped next to a tree to watch.

He was fine, and he smiled, despite knowing I was checking up on him.

But I couldn't help it.

The man was mine, and that's what good girlfriends did, right?

I'm okay.

I bit my lip.

You better be, Mister. You also have a lot of explainin' to do.

His lips quirked up into a small smile before I turned around and got back to work.

I started taking pictures, and it wasn't until about forty-five minutes into the session that Leyland finally joined in the shoot.

I didn't comment when he stiffly joined in, and it wasn't until I said something funny that he finally cracked a smile.

Things after that were about as smooth as they could be with Ian watching my every move, and I would've said they were even enjoyable.

"All right," I told the bride, Candace. "These will be done by next weekend, tops. If I get them done earlier, I'll upload the finals to my website and you can download them from the site directly to your computer. Is there a certain shot you want me to work on first?"

She shook her head.

"No," she stopped when her groom butted in. "One with the kids," he said. "All of us together."

I nodded my head, a small smile overtaking my face.

"I can do that. I'll tag you on Facebook with it, and likely another closer to the end of the week. Sound good?" I asked the two of them.

One of their kids, the smaller ones that looked to be about four, screamed shrilly.

"Mommy, a dragon!" he cried out.

I looked up and nearly grinned when I saw Mace, obviously enjoying the hell out of the attention he was garnering from all the patrons in the Dallas Memorial Park, flying low for all to see.

"What is that about?" I muttered to Ian, who'd come up behind me.

"He's a showoff sometimes," he said. "And he could shield himself, but dragons are popular among this park since it's close to The Heart. They're spotted around here often."

"Ahh," I murmured, just as much enthralled with him flying around as the rest of the patrons were. "He looks like he's flying kind of low. Does he normally do that?"

Ian was about to reply when Mace suddenly banked hard right, causing everyone to gasp.

That's when we saw the first hook attached to a rope come flying out of the air from behind a large boulder.

Then another, and another.

Ian went from completely relaxed to wired in a little over ten seconds.

CHAPTER 16

Wink's moods don't just 'swing.' They pivot, twirl, thrash, and swivel.
-Ian's secret thoughts

Ian

Shield!

One second Mace was flying in the air for all to see, and the next he wasn't.

I breathed a sigh of relief, but it was cut short when something came sailing toward me next.

Using my own ability to shield through Mace, I cursed and dropped to the ground, taking Wink with me.

"Don't. Move," I ordered softly. "The shield works best when you don't move or talk."

She stared at me like I was crazy, almost as if to say 'then why are you talking?'

Grinning, I chanced a look up and saw a man walking toward us.

"That's him," I whispered. "That's the guy. The one that can hide his aura."

"What guy?" she asked just barely loud enough so I could hear it, looking around as she tried to figure out who I was talking to.

"She doesn't see me," the man said. "Only you can."

I stiffened and moved until Wink could move.

"Who are you?" I asked stiffly, trying to put Wink behind me at the same time as I was trying to stand and project my voice away from where I was actually standing.

The man watched me move, as if he could see through the veil.

I knew he couldn't see me. He was talking to me, but his eyes were watching to the right of me.

So, although he had a vague idea of where I was at, he wouldn't be able to get us as long as we stayed quiet and moved slowly to the left of where we'd been.

"Tell Keifer that he's been warned," the man said.

I squeezed Wink's hand.

Stop. Stay.

She stayed, and I could tell she wasn't very happy to be staying where I left her.

Complain she did not. Happy she was not. Obedient she was. *For once.*

Once I was far enough away, I urged her in the opposite direction I was standing in.

Good girl. Keep moving toward Mace and I'll meet you there.

She lifted her lip in a silent snarl, then started to back away, using the chaos of the crowd making their way to the parking lot as a cover as she moved.

"Why would I warn Keifer? I don't even know what to warn him about," I replied, then moved two giant strides in the opposite direction.

I probably looked like a dumbass as I moved in such an erratic pattern, but I didn't know who this guy was from Adam. I wasn't going to give him a voice tag of where I was so he could use whatever powers I knew he had on me.

The man's eyes narrowed on the spot I used to be in, and then he subtly lifted his right hand.

I could feel it—energy of some sort—as it passed me.

It felt like a gust of wind as it moved in the direction I'd once been in, and I knew my instincts that told me to move were right.

Take a picture of him.

I didn't wait around for him to tell me anything more. I wouldn't be stupid and wait around while he did God knew what to me.

Keifer wasn't the only person I had to worry about anymore. He wasn't the most important thing in my life. Wink was.

"Keifer is my…" the man whipped his head around, staring narrow eyed in the direction of Mace and Wink.

I picked up a large boulder off the ground, one that was used as decoration for the ugly water attraction that Wink had used as a backdrop for a few of her pictures, hefted its weight in my hand, and launched it at the man.

It wasn't a light throw, either.

In fact, I'd put everything I had in that throw.

And the man fucking caught it.

Right out of the air.

Then launched it right back at me with twice the force and three times the speed.

I had just enough time to lift my hand to block the rock from hitting me directly in the face, and pain shot through my entire arm.

So much pain that it doubled me over and stole my breath.

Bone crunched, and blood started to flow from the wound of the rock's collision with my arm. It took everything I had to keep myself upright as I moved in a hunched over position toward Wink.

Mace, being the awesome creature he was, moved toward me, intercepting me about halfway and lifting me onto his back.

"Go," I coughed.

Mace went, and the last thing I saw before the pain of my crushed arm stole my ability to stay aware was the man watching us go.

With a mother fucking smile on his face.

***

"What'd he look like?" Keifer sat back in his office chair and kicked his feet up, resting them on the edge of his huge black wooden desk.

My eyes flickered around the room, taking in Derek with his stoic, disbelieving eyes. Jean Luc—who was there, but not really there.

That, likely, had a lot to do with my sister.

My sister who, when I'd talked to her on the phone earlier about her house, had made mention of Jean Luc not just once, but over ten times.

Then there was Nikolai and his wife, Brooklyn, who was sitting on his lap.

Blythe was sitting on the desk next to Keifer's feet, watching me warily, waiting for me to speak.

"Tall. Black hair that hung down around past his eyes. Green eyes. Olive complexion. Scar on his right cheek," Wink rattled off. "He was like a Keanu Reeves lookalike."

Keifer grunted.

"What could he do?" Blythe asked, rocking back and forth from one foot to another.

I lifted up my newly healed arm—thanks to my woman—and pointed at it. "Strength. Echo fucking location. I don't know. He could guesstimate where we were standing even when I had my shield up."

"Fuck me," Keifer growled. "Nikolai, any luck with the photo?"

"I'm trying to sharpen the image, but until I can do that, all it looks like to me is Keanu Reeves," Nikolai replied.

Blythe snorted as did Nikolai's woman.

"That's not helping, brother," Keifer retorted.

Suddenly, Brooklyn jumped up from her husband's lap, clapping loudly, and bringing everyone's attention to her.

"That's the guy…" Brooklyn's face bunched as she thought. "That's the guy from the cabin, I think. I don't remember a lot, but I remember him. His face. And from what I'm getting when you project the info at me…it's his voice that I remember the most."

In conjunction with my own powers, Nikolai and Brooklyn were able to figure out that I could project the memories I gathered from the things that I touched—and saw—to their minds.

We hadn't figured out how to project them to others besides them yet, but in time, I believed we would figure it out.

"That's all I got," she grumbled.

"And that doesn't help me," I agreed. "I've been spending the last few months trying to learn whatever I can about that man. I even took Wink to the cabin to see if she could get anything that I wasn't able to myself."

"I wasn't able to see anything that he didn't see," she looked at Brooklyn guiltily. "And I didn't even see his face. Only a hint of what he might look like."

I patted her back.

"She understands," I said softly.

Brooklyn nodded.

"Nothing that happened to me in there isn't already common knowledge," Brooklyn shared. "Go ahead and share if you feel you need to."

I squeezed Wink's hip, and she looked at me.

"That man...," she swallowed. "I only got impressions of him. Feelings, the same as Ian. We're only able to go with what you are saying about the man's appearance. Do you mind if we touch you?"

"Kinky," Nikolai drawled.

Brooklyn thumped Nikolai in the chest with her hand, then walked over and placed her hand out, waiting for us both to touch it.

I grabbed her wrist while Wink grabbed her hand.

"What you're going to want to do is think about the memory," I instructed. "Otherwise everything we get off you will be whatever happens to be up first. And it could take years."

Brooklyn snorted, but closed her eyes and concentrated.

At first I only got tiny trickles.

Dragon riders and their mates were inherently good shielders. They could hide what they didn't want to be common knowledge without actively doing so.

Which was why at first I was only getting trickles.

"Nikolai," I opened my eyes. "If you don't mind, will you touch her? I need her shields to come down to allow us to access what she's trying to show us."

"Now it's really getting kinky," Nikolai teased.

My brows lifted when he stood, but he didn't touch her anywhere. He wrapped her up in his arms and buried his face into her neck.

The moment his skin was touching hers, all of Brooklyn's walls came down, and her world swirled and merged into ours.

***

My head started to pound as my body became more aware of the pain I was in.

However, my attempt to use my veil had worked, and I disappeared from sight only moments later.

Rolling to my feet, I gritted my teeth against the pain in my arm and moved to the door, freezing when a man stopped in front of it, blocking my exit.

The man was tall with dark black hair, a scar that ran the length of his jaw, and a wiry whipcord look to him. Almost as if he was a runner—a runner who didn't eat enough before he worked his ass off.

"She's around here somewhere," the man said. "You need to get up off your ass and find her."

That was directed towards my brother. Stupid asshole.

I was happy to see him still writhing in pain on the ground, almost gleeful in fact.

"Seriously?" the man asked. "What do I pay you for?"

Josiah grimaced in pain and lifted his knees up under his torso before pushing up to his haunches.

"Kill her," he said gravely. "Fucking kill her. She's ruined my life; she doesn't deserve to live."

How in the hell had I ruined his life?

I took a step backward and stepped wrong, bumping the small table at my side.

My hand automatically went out to stop the lamp from falling, but it was the one that had been broken upon my arrival, meaning I screamed.

Letting the lamp drop to the ground, I limped, slightly hunched over, to the side of the room, directly behind where my brother had managed to get to his feet, albeit pitifully.

My brother looked around the room frantically, almost as if he was waiting for me to bean him over the head any second.

And, technically, I would have...if I had something to use.

I wasn't sure I could lift anything at this moment in time.

Instead, I sank down to my butt, letting my back slide against the wall until my backside met the cool tiled floor.

"Listen, Robert," Josiah said, a slight wheeze in his voice. "She's not going to leave. Not with knowing who all is here. Let's just get the good stuff started. She'll show herself when she sees what we're doing. She's a nurse. Don't they take oaths or something?"

I gritted my teeth and let my head fall down to my knees, my broken arm dangling uselessly at my side.

"Fine," ugly Robert said. "I've got my stuff right here. I'll take the geis off of him; you can see how to do it for next time."

My eyes widened in shock as they walked over to Merrick and picked him up by the arms, half dragging, half carrying him to the kitchen table that was only a few feet from my face.

***

"Robert," I said. "His name is Robert?"

"Who's Merrick?" Wink asked.

Brooklyn stiffened and Nikolai patted her cheek.

"Merrick is the man who tried to kidnap me," Brooklyn swallowed. "That little snippet that you just saw was actually Robert—the man you saw in the park—taking the geis off of Merrick. The problem with that is that the geis was tied to his life force."

"And he died?" Wink asked in confusion.

Brooklyn's eyes flicked to mine once before returning to Wink's.

"No, Ian was able to save him."

"Then where's he at?" Wink asked.

"That…is a very good fucking question," Keifer joined the party. "One that I'd love to know the answer to."

I picked up a paperweight off of Keifer's desk, tossing it into my other hand as I watched Keifer.

Then froze as my world, for the second time in five minutes, warped.

And when I finally came to, nothing was the same.

CHAPTER 17

*A wise man once said, 'Fuck this shit' and lived happily ever after.
-Ian's secret thoughts*

Ian

"This is the last time you go anywhere without a trio of guards on your ass," I informed her bluntly. "I almost made a fatal mistake today, and I knew beforehand that I should be careful. I don't know what made me say yes, but it definitely has something to do with the way you shoved your vagina in my face when you asked me if you could do the session."

She giggled, rolling over until her face was buried in my arm.

"I don't remember that being a problem at the time," she murmured.

I could tell she was now looking at me, her eyes studying my face.

"You picked something up today while you were at Keifer's."

I nodded my head. "I did."

"What was it?" she whispered.

"Farrow."

"What about Farrow?" she persisted.

I swallowed.

"Farrow's not so good anymore," I said through parched lips. "What I saw today, if it's true…it could be bad."

She sat up and I could feel her breathing on my face.

"What did you see," she asked again, poking me in the chest and booking no room for argument.

I sighed and pulled her completely on top of me, wrapping my arms around her back and timing my breaths to hers.

She felt so good against my chest.

So good.

Nothing would make what I was about to say any easier, but I had to say it.

Had to get it off my chest.

"I only saw enough to really suspect," I cleared my throat. "But if what I suspect is true, then Keifer's going to flip his lid."

She poked me in the ribs, and I chuckled.

My erection, never one to go down when she was near me, jerked against her.

She wiggled, but said or did nothing more as she waited for me to finish.

I squeezed her hips.

"Farrow is selling secrets."

"Selling what kind of secrets?" she growled. "If you don't give me the whole damn story, I'm going over to Keifer's house, walking inside, and heading straight for that paperweight."

I chuckled against her.

"You don't have to walk over there. I took it," I told her. "It's in my pants pocket."

She was gone so quick I didn't even have time to hold on.

I heard her shuffling around the darkened room, and I took pity on her and rolled, switching on the lamp beside the bed.

I nearly laughed as I saw her on her hands and knees as she searched blindly for my pants.

The moment the light lit the room, she darted for my pants and yanked the paperweight out, gasping the moment it touched her skin.

I knew what she was seeing.

Farrow, walking into the room. Picking up paperweights as he tried to find the key to Keifer's desk. He picked up the last paperweight, then set it down with a loud thump.

When he set it down, though, he accidentally knocked over the cup of water that was sitting on the side of the desk.

Instead of the water flowing off the side, it flowed to the middle.

Farrow, in his haste to stop the water from getting the paper wet, hastily tore his shirt off and sopped up the water, dislodging the jar of pens that was at the corner of the desk.

And spilling out not just the pens, but the key that he'd been searching for.

Once he had the key, he opened the desk and started to sift through files.

The thing about that, though, was that he knew what he was looking for. Knew what was in there. What was good, and what wasn't.

After taking five files, he locked the desk back up.

Just before he was able to clean the desk, he heard him. Keifer. Walking swiftly to the entrance of the office.

He hastily grabbed his shirt, then ran as quietly as he could to the corner of the room and waited.

Keifer entered, took one look at the desk, and then roared.

"Blythe! Your fucking cat was in my office again!" Keifer had yelled.

With his head studying his desk with resignation, Farrow had slipped from the room with an armful of files, and a sneer covering his face.

"So you think he's taking these files to someone?" she asked me, placing the paperweight on the nightstand and climbing back in bed.

I held the covers to the side, urged her to retake her position by patting my lap, and waited for her to follow my directions.

She did so without a fight, walking across the bed on her knees before straddling my thighs.

"I don't know what he plans to do with the files," I admitted. "I can guess, though, but I won't know for sure what he planned to do with them until I ask him."

She blinked. "Ask him."

I nodded.

"Farrow seems to be that kid that everyone babies. What's the deal with him? Why is he not held to the same standard as everyone else?" Wink asked, crossing her arms over her chest.

I knew what she was asking.

Farrow didn't work. Farrow didn't do any reconnaissance like the rest of the dragon riders. Farrow didn't do anything. When the others did stints of patrols, Farrow wasn't factored into the list.

"Farrow isn't like the other dragon riders."

"Why?" she asked shortly, tired of my evasive answers.

"Farrow was the baby. He didn't have the same upbringing that Nikolai and Keifer did," I cleared my throat.

"Neither did you," Wink pointed out, running her hand down my chest. "But that didn't turn you into an asshole."

I laughed. "Thank you, baby." I let my hands trail up the tops of her thighs. "Farrow saved my life."

"Why?" she asked. "How?"

I let my eyes move up to hers.

"I was in a bad place," I said. "I was steadily drinking myself to death when Farrow found me, and then dragged his brother back to me. Keifer forced me to get my shit together."

Wink grinned.

"He seems like the type to do that."

"He is," I agreed. "And so I continue to work with the dragon riders, trying to repay my debt."

"You don't want to be here?" she asked curiously.

"At times, no. I'd rather just live my life. This life—one as a dragon rider—it's dangerous." I started wrapping her hands around my fist. "And what I hate the most is that I have to go away from you. Your time is stolen from me, and I don't fucking like it."

With that pronouncement, I pulled her hair back and exposed her neck to my tongue.

"And I don't like not being able to have you anytime I want."

Her eyes dilated as my words slammed into her, making themselves at home in her mind, burrowing deep in her synapses, letting me in exactly where I wanted to be.

"I fucking love you, woman," I growled, rolling until she was underneath me. "I've loved you for fucking ever. You've brought my sister back to me. You've made me seem almost human in the eyes of the other dragon riders. And you have my back. I don't know what I'd do without you."

Her eyes filled with tears.

"Does that mean you're going to marry me and make it all legal in the eyes of the law?" she asked roughly.

I placed my hand on her neck, wrapping my fingers around her throat, exactly where the mating tattoo was located.

She followed suit, placing her hand on my neck, directly over the tattoo on me.

I yanked her panties down her legs, not caring in the least that they ripped in my haste to get to her pussy.

"Fuck," she gasped, her legs parting automatically the moment they were free of the constricting fabric.

I fell in between her splayed thighs, notching my hips with hers.

The hard ridge of my erection pressed against the lips of her sex.

"What do you think about kids?" I asked.

Her eyes widened.

"I'm not ready for kids," she swallowed. "I want them…just not yet."

I continued to stare at her, and she swallowed.

"I don't want kids yet," she said again.

The longer I stared at her, the more uncomfortable she got.

I could read her mind.

I knew for a fact that she wanted kids. I could read the thoughts as they flittered through her mind like multiple hummingbirds trying to fly around the small area at once.

"Wink," I brought my free hand up to cup her face. "What's the problem?"

"Can we talk about this later?" she pleaded, her thoughts coming too fast now for me to read them before the next one came.

I studied her face, took in her eyes and her desperate expression, and then nodded my head once.

"Yeah, I can do that." I murmured. "But one day, I'm going to get this vasectomy reversed. All I need is your opinion on the matter."

She didn't have anything to reply.

CHAPTER 18

A day without coffee is like…just kidding. I have no idea.
-Wink's secret thoughts

Wink

I stared at the pregnancy test, vomit already starting to make its way back up my esophagus even after I'd spent the last two hours throwing up.

You need to tell him, Mace chastised me gently. *He won't be mad.*

I moaned in frustration.

I know. He's too good for me.

He was, too.

I didn't deserve him. A man like Ian deserved the world and I'd ruined mine.

I'd lied to him today.

The man I'd seen in the park.

I knew him.

I knew him well.

In the biblical sense, too.

Oh, god.

The baby I was carrying could be Robert's. Or it could be Ian's. I knew that just like I knew that whatever was going on right now, that it was going to be bad.

I'd slept with the man one time, and one time only.

Shane had introduced me to him at a party, and I'd instantly found a connection in the man. He was attractive, funny, and a good friend of Shane's. I'd seen him around quite a bit at Shane's bar, as well as at other parties.

It'd been my first ever one-night stand, and I wasn't sure, afterward, just what I'd done.

The sex had been okay, sure.

Nothing like what I had with Ian, but the man hadn't been a slacker, either.

We'd both gotten off, I'd left the hotel room, and I'd never seen him again.

Until today.

Eight weeks later.

Six of which I'd been with Ian.

I was a slut!

"You're not a slut," Ian said, startling me.

I gasped and turned, losing purchase on the toilet bowl and falling to my knees in front of him.

"You're making yourself sick," he said, bending down so he could pick me up, one arm going underneath my knees and the other going behind my back.

I started crying.

"You know?" I whispered dejectedly.

"Yes," he confirmed. "I've known you were pregnant for a month."

My mouth fell open.

"What?" she gasped. "How? I didn't even know."

He looked at me.

"I can see DNA, honey," he told me gently. "Your DNA and the baby's DNA are different enough that it's easy to see."

My eyes closed as his words poured over me like a soothing balm.

"I've been trying to figure out how to tell you for a week," I whispered, my eyes opening to catch his. "You've known for all this time and haven't called me on it yet?"

He smoothed his hand down my hair that was falling every which way out of my sloppy bun on top of my head.

"I've known you were pregnant," he hesitated. "I didn't tell you I knew because it seemed like you were still processing it in your head." He smiled then. "I probably would've let you tell me, but then you started losing weight because you were worrying yourself sick over what I'd say or do."

"Who are you and what have you done with Ian?" I challenged him.

He snorted and placed me on the bed, immediately bending to the floor and picking up my flip flops.

"I have a problem at the mill, and I need to go check on it." He slipped on a flip flop. "You can either come with me, or go to the sanctuary with Brooklyn and Blythe."

I pursed my lips.

"How long will you be there?" I asked. "All day, like two days ago?"

He shook his head. "Not that I know of. Should be a quick in and out. Something is wrong with the planer. Not that I can fix it, though. I'll have to call in the repair company."

I eyed him suspiciously.

"You're being awfully nonchalant about this…"

Four hours later, I was twiddling my thumbs on the stupid brown stool across from Ian, who was on his back underneath the biggest machine I'd ever seen.

I'd peed twice, searched through the empty refrigerator three times, and had taken no less than ten laps around the huge shop.

Now, I was literally bored out of my mind.

"Ian."

"What?" he grunted, his large muscles bulging.

"What time are we looking at now?" I pushed.

He growled something at me that I couldn't quite understand, but the mental picture came through loud and clear.

He wanted me to leave him alone.

Smothering a grin, I got up and started walking to the front room, looking outside and contemplating making a run for it.

Then I saw Mace.

Hey, Ian.

His growled—even through mind speak— answer was quite hilarious.

What do you want, demon?

I really did giggle this time as I watched Mace bring one clawed large paw to the earth and dig it into the grass, spreading his claws in the soft grass like a cat would when it was kneading your skin.

Can Mace fly me to McDonald's?

And what, take you through the drive-through? he sighed. *I think not.*

Just wait a few more minutes and I'll be done.

The only person I could blame for the next lapse in judgement was me.

I chose to walk out the door, not realizing that danger awaited outside.

I'd only intended to talk to Mace, yet the moment I stepped foot outside the door something fucking snapped inside of me, and all that made me, me, was gone.

Luckily, or unluckily for me, Mace got to come with.

CHAPTER 19

Going to Target with Wink is about as much fun as going to a bar with my AA sponsor.
-Ian's secret thoughts

Ian

I felt it the moment she was gone.

One second she was standing right outside the front door, and the next she wasn't.

Her mind seemed to just disappear, appearing as if she never existed at all.

I'd just gotten to my feet, when, suddenly, I couldn't figure out what the hell I was doing down there in the first place.

My body swayed, and it didn't take long before I was on my knees with my head in my hands.

A scuffle from my right had me lifting my head, my eyes taking in who was in the doorway.

"Hello?" I called.

An old man appeared in the doorway to the large room I was standing in, and it took me a moment to place him.

"Eldridge?" I asked in confusion. "I thought you had today off."

My mind, which only moments ago was clear, was now confused and cottony like something had clouded my brain. Alcohol or something.

Mr. Eldridge looked at me like I'd said something amusing.

"You're forgetting already?" he asked.

"Forgetting what?"

"Forgetting what should never be forgotten."

Then, just like that, he was gone as if he'd never fucking been there in the first place.

"Fuckin' crazy old man," I mumbled, pushing myself up to my feet.

My body started to sway, but I stiffened my spine and put one foot in front of the other, heading to the bathroom.

Except the bathroom wasn't where it was supposed to be.

What I thought was the bathroom had morphed into a fucking kitchen, and what used to be an old storage closet I could tell was now the bathroom.

"What the fuck is going on?" I yelled, looking around the space.

I'd never once seen it before.

Was I in the right place?

When nobody answered my bellowed question, I made my way to the bathroom and immediately headed to the sink, turned it on, and then cupped my hand under the faucet to gather water.

The moment the cool water touched my face, I felt something shift. Something that I knew I'd forgotten.

The cobwebs cleared, and a soft flash of strawberry blonde hair flashed through my brain before it was gone as if it'd never been.

I looked up, staring at my eyes in the mirror, and instantly flinched.

My eyes had lines that weren't supposed to be there.

My face had fucking hair!

I had a goddamned beard!

Then my eyes lit on the…*tattoo?*…on my neck.

Since when did I have a tattoo?

"Ian?" someone, a woman, called from the other room.

My hand resting on the small handprint on my neck, I whirled around and stared at my sister.

My sister…my aged sister. She must've been twenty years older, but I knew it was her. I would know her beautiful face and gorgeous eyes anywhere.

"Can I help you?"

I acted like I didn't know her, but I knew she knew it was me.

"Why are you talking to me like that?" she asked. "You were the one to tell me to meet you here. For the life of me I can't figure out why, though. I haven't seen you since I was fifteen. Why do I know where you are?"

"What day is it?" I asked her.

She pursed her lips.

"Umm…" she hesitated. "I have no idea."

My eyes went around the office, looking for a calendar of some sort like Old Eldridge used to hang on the wall, but I didn't find a damn thing on the wall but a single picture.

And what I saw in that picture made my heart stop.

My sister looked at me.

"I think we're missing something here." She looked at the picture, shoulder rubbing my shoulder.

"That's…" I strained to come up with a name for the woman wrapped around me in the picture, and couldn't. "I don't know. She's mine, though. That much I can tell."

"Then where is she?" my sister countered.

I shook my head, unable to come up with a plausible answer.

"I'm fucking lost, and I don't know where to look, or what to do."

That's when the whole goddamned building shook, and I ran outside just in time to see the mill's entire fucking parking lot fill with dragons.

I stared at the large, dark headed man, wondering what in the hell I'd done now.

My sister, not one to back down from a fight, grabbed hold of my hand.

It didn't matter that I was only just now seeing her after years upon years apart.

She knew I would protect her, just as easily as I knew that if it came down to a fight, she'd be at my back the whole way.

But the man now dismounting his dragon didn't mean us harm.

There was something about him, though, that was calling to me.

Not in a weird way, either.

In one that felt right.

"Who are you?" I asked him.

He stared at me.

"You don't know me?" he asked.

I shook my head.

"No."

"I don't know you, either," he admitted.

My brows rose.

"But something led us here, so we're here," he continued. "Now we need to figure out why."

CHAPTER 20

Despite being a pain in the ass, you have to admit that I bring a lot to the table.
-Text from Wink to Ian

Ian

It took us two days to figure out why.

The entire forty-eight hours had been harrowing to say the least.

We'd stayed on the grounds of the mill, and that'd been our biggest mistake.

A, because when we were on the grounds of the mill, that also meant that we were detached from the world. No cell phone coverage. No phones. No television.

Old man Eldridge didn't believe in modern amenities. When he came to work, he expected to be at work. There was no taking away from work, either. Not even emergency phone calls.

If they need us, they'll send a car. If they don't, then they don't need us.

B, because something was draining us. Something was making it to where we were weak, and all of us but a select few were literally too weak to move.

I'd been getting sicker and sicker since, too.

It hadn't started off that way, but by the time the forty-eighth hour passed, I was becoming lethargic and I could barely stand.

"We need to get him to a doctor," someone said in a thick Cajun accent.

My eyes followed the sound of that voice, and I stared across the apartment like office at the man who'd said that.

Jean Luc.

I didn't know him.

Hell, I didn't know any of these men.

But our bond, one I knew we shared, pulsed inside of me.

I had some sort of connection to them, and that was keeping me from kicking them all the hell out of my mill.

Especially since they seemed just as confused as I was on where they were supposed to be.

It was as if the last ten years of our lives had been erased.

Poof, gone like a snap of the fingers.

"We're not going anywhere," Keifer said. "There's something here that fucked us the moment we entered the parking lot, and we're going to find it. You know it, and I know it."

The big man was sitting down on the couch across from me, his head hanging loosely between his arms that were resting on his knees.

His eyes were on the floor, and it was more than obvious, even by my sick eyes, that something was wrong with him.

He wasn't, however, at my level yet. Nor the level of his brother, which was in the recliner directly next to mine.

"Listen, Keifer," Derek, another of the men that'd shown up, said. "You know, as well as I do, that something more is at stake here than we're both realizing. We need to get out of this place and head for your shop or something."

"I'm okay," I sat up, slowly, and looked around the room.

"No, you're not." Keifer shot back. "But we can agree to disagree."

I swallowed and stood up, a wave of nausea taking over my belly.

I hadn't eaten in well over forty hours, nor had I drank anything.

Likely that was all that was wrong with me, but the idea of anything to eat or drink was enough to make my stomach heave.

"I'm going outside for a few," I gritted out, pushing through the door.

The moment I stepped outside, the feeling in my belly got worse.

So much worse, in fact, that I nearly turned and went back to the chair.

The only thing moving me forward at this point was sheer force of will.

Something was wrong.

Every time I closed my eyes, I saw the strawberry blonde from the picture. I saw flashes of memories that were literally making me crave something I had no clue how to find.

"Ian?" a soft voice called.

I turned the corner and found my sister there, leaning against the building.

"Hey, Buttercup," I called roughly. "What are you doing outside by yourself for?"

She smiled sadly at me.

"I'm confused," she whispered.

I leaned against the metal side of the mill and looked at her.

She'd grown up to be beautiful.

Every time I looked at her my heart constricted.

She looked just like our mom used to look.

"Confused about what?" I questioned.

She turned to look at the chain link fence that separated the mill's property from the corn field on the other side of the fence.

"Why you left," she whispered. "Why you're back? Why you let me think you were dead all this time? You had a cop tell my foster parents that you died."

I closed my eyes.

"I knew you weren't dead, you know." She picked up a gravel rock next to her thighs that were lying out straight in front of her, and tossed it at the fence.

It struck the metal with a soft ping, and she did it again.

"I wanted you to have what I couldn't," I said. "There was someone that wanted you. Not me. When they said that they found a home for you, I was happy. I would've killed you, and we both know it."

She picked up another rock, and my eyes lit on the drain spout that was directly beside my foot.

"I had a good life," she said. "They paid for my college. And are *still* paying for my college."

Mattie was in school again, this time to get her masters degree. I was so fucking proud of her and everything that she accomplished.

I tapped the drain spout with my booted foot, and blinked when something that looked like a crow's foot fell out of it.

"I know they are, because I'm forwarding the money for it to your foster parents," I admitted. "I follow you to school sometimes just to make sure you're happy. I went to your graduations—high school, associates, and your bachelors. I went to your prom and saw you walk down the stage with your boyfriend at the time."

"I know that, too," she said, picking up the crow's foot and holding it between two pinched fingers. "I know I have more questions for you, but my brain feels fuzzy." She bent forward to pick up the black thing that'd fallen from the downspout. "What the hell is this?"

I picked the thing up, and letters started to swirl in my mind.

Unconsciously, my hand tightened down on the little trinket, and the brittle thing snapped, cracking completely in half.

Then, without me doing a damn thing, a light pink trajectory started to filter through the air, like a trail of some sort.

And then more things started to drift through my head.

A sense of urgency.

Panic.

Pain.

Fear.

All of the bad things that one never wants to experience by themselves, coursed through me all at once.

And I exploded.

CHAPTER 21

Why is there a '9' setting on the toaster? Who likes their toast to be charred?
-Text from Wink to Ian

Wink

I knew the moment he realized everything. The very second he realized that I was gone, and I'd been gone for some time.

It'd been the worst forty-eight hours of my life, and I was fairly sure that if I made it through the next hour, then I'd live.

But the next hour was likely going to kill me.

I never once doubted that Ian would realize what was going on. I never once thought he'd not be able to beat whatever Robert had done to keep him in the dark.

I'd woken up chained to a bed, luckily still fully clothed, with Robert pacing the room behind me.

"What were you doing there?" Robert asked again.

I was shaking my head in confusion. "I don't know what you're talking about, Robert. I was where I was supposed to be."

"This wasn't how this was supposed to go. I was to take the healer, according to the files. He's the weak link. Once the healer is gone, everything else goes according to plan. With nobody to heal the injuries, everyone dies. No heart equals no life. No life can only happen if the healer is gone. You were not supposed to be there," Robert continued to pace.

He had some sort of foot in his hand.

A chicken foot or something.

I couldn't really tell from flat on my back on the bed.

I had to pee like a race horse, and I knew any moment I was going to lose the battle with my bladder. It'd been hours.

"Robert, I have to pee," I said. "I need you to untie me so I can go to the bathroom."

He stared at me with annoyance. "There's a water proof sheet on the bed."

He looked around at the one room cabin, the same one that Ian had bought after Brooklyn had been found after her kidnapping.

"Robert, please?"

"No," he refused.

I couldn't believe the balls that Robert had.

He trusted his spell, or whatever the fuck he'd done, so much that it never even occurred to him that Ian would get out of whatever he was put under.

He's stupid.

Ian's voice back in my mind had me breathing deeply for the first time in two whole days.

Where the hell have you been?

The screech couldn't be helped.

I literally was at the point of breaking, and the only thing making me remain calm was the fact that I had another life to think about beside mine.

A life that I could feel losing its fight with each second that passed.

My body was shutting down.

The longer I was away from Ian, the more energy that left my body.

I'm coming. Hold on, I'm coming.

The only thing that'd saved the baby at this point was the fact that we were so close to The Heart, the very thing that Ian had used to help save the others not too long ago.

Twenty minutes passed, and I was just deciding that I would indeed have to pee on myself, when I felt the sudden change.

It was subtle, yes, but I felt it nonetheless.

At first I wasn't quite sure what it was, but the longer I sat there, the longer it took me to realize that someone was in the room with me.

A man.

Nikolai.

The touch of his hand against mine had me automatically closing my eyes and trying to read the traces of DNA that he'd left on my skin when he'd touched me.

I'd opened my eyes and looked across the room at Robert, who was still pacing the room.

"Robert, please," I begged. "I don't want to pee on myself. Please."

He looked over at me.

"Please," I persisted.

He sighed and walked toward me.

"I'm going to untie you from the bed, but you're going to leave the ropes tied to your wrist. There will be absolutely no fooling around. If I even think that something is going wrong, I'll crush you." He proved his fact by holding the foot up that he'd been holding since I got here, and giving it a little shake.

The moment he shook it, my entire body convulsed as if I'd been electrocuted.

I stared numbly at the stupid foot, and realized then why he was holding it, and had never let it go in over forty-eight hours. *It was tied to me.*

 Like a fucking voodoo doll.

"Do you understand me?" he asked viciously.

I nodded my head, not wanting him any closer than he already was.

The man scared me.

He was a freakin' psycho.

How I could have ever slept with this man, I didn't know.

Though I hadn't told Ian that little tidbit.

I hadn't been able to work up the courage.

He'd been so understanding about knowing about the child that wasn't his.

If he'd realized just who the man was to me that'd gotten me pregnant, then he'd have had a shit fit. I still couldn't believe my freakin' luck.

How could you have been so stupid? How could you have done this to yourself and Ian? You've doomed yourself and your baby!

The words in my head wouldn't stop, and it was getting to the point where if I wasn't careful, Ian would hear every stray thought that I had.

Shut up! I snapped at myself. *I know I need to. But he doesn't need to know right now. Not when we've spent the last forty-eight hours apart*

Oh, My Dragon

and he's trying to figure out how the hell to get me out of this.

Something's wrong. Ian's tense voice filled my mind. *What is it?*

He's untying me and letting me go to the bathroom. He has this foot of some sort in his hand that's somehow controls my every action if he wills it to...kind of like a voodoo doll. Whatever he does to the token, happens to me. The moment I get out of hand, or do something he doesn't like, he could hurt me. Greatly.

Ian's curse was loud in the forefront of my mind, but I didn't let that deter me. I would be leaving.

I didn't care if he broke me the moment he realized I was gone. It didn't matter anyway. If I didn't get next to Ian soon, I'd die.

That was what I'd read in the book he'd so kindly provided for me. The book that was written by the previous king, for his sons, who would one day find their chosen mates.

The female is fed by the male's connection to the dragon. The two mates will forever have to be within the vicinity of the other, or they start to grow weak and eventually die if the separation goes on too long. Never stay apart for more than twenty-four hours. Trust me, it doesn't go away. I know.

That was it, word for word, from the book. Those were the words that kept repeating in my mind the entire time we'd been separated. Each moment we'd been apart, the weaker I grew.

I never had a chance at leaving Ian. Even if I'd wanted to—which I didn't. We were meant to be together, and would be for the rest of our lives…or we'd be dead.

Which was a scary notion. We were still in Dallas. Ian's shop was in Dallas. We were in the same freakin' city!

Should it really have been that bad?

Yes. Mace's clear understanding of the matter filled my head. *Because if you're not together, then the bond is not as strong as it needs to be.*

What do you mean? I asked him, freezing at the sink where I'd begun to slowly and methodically wash my hands.

The entire point of destined mates is to have them feed off of each other. To make them stronger when they're together. They're meant to ride into battle together, not apart.

My brows rose.

That would be the total opposite of what I've witnessed between all the mated pairs so far. Keifer, Nikolai and Ian would never allow their wives to ride into battle with them.

Mace's curse had me freezing.

And they would die if the threat were great enough.

My brows rose.

Explain.

Story and Declan. They're formidable on their own, but together…they're unstoppable. Each and every dragon rider and their mate—if they've found their mate, could have something similar to that. There are very few mated pairs left in this world, and the only mated pair we have at our sanctuary is Story and Declan.

How do you know so much about this? I asked.

Sadness filled Mace's mind. But before I could read any more into it, he shut his thoughts down viciously.

So fast and quick that it literally hurt my brain to feel.

You were mated? I asked softly, my heart breaking for him.

I was. The cold, formal aristocratic tone of his voice made me wince. He only took on that tone when he was extremely pissed. And I hadn't heard him slip into formal mode the entire time we'd been captive. But for his mate…for his mate he had and that was devastating.

I debated whether to ask my next question, but he beat me to it.

Daya was taken from me sixteen years, eleven months, and twenty-nine days ago.

I closed my eyes.

How are you still alive?

Dragons are different than dragon riders. Where riders grow weak without their mates, dragons grow stronger. We share a single life force, and when one drops off that force, the remaining dragon gets the entirety of the force they shared. It's almost as if the departed mate pushes their share to their mate to give them a fighting chance without them. Mace explained.

Oh, God. That was terrible. Absolutely terrible.

I'm so sorry, Mace.

Nothing you can do, little one. It's my burden to bear. I'm just telling you so you understand the dynamics of mating. If you worked together, instead of separately, life would be much different for all the mated pairs.

I took his words to heart as I finally finished washing my hands.

Once they were clean of the dirt and grime, I used the restroom, and then rewashed my hands.

The moment I'd finished, I startled when I saw Nikolai standing in front of the shower.

My mouth dropped open at seeing him standing there.

He held up his hand in a silent order to stay, pointed at the closed toilet seat, and then mouthed 'sit.'

So I did, and then he disappeared before I could even think of something to say.

Had he watched me pee?

He didn't watch you pee, Wink. Ian's amused voice filled my ears. *He did, however, instruct you to stay. He's going to weave an illusion that should enable me to come in and get that thing he's using to control you. When I have it, he'll give us enough time to get out.*

Mace's tied up in the...

I have him. He's safe.

Breathing a sigh of relief, I took a deep breath of air when suddenly I wasn't where I was supposed to be anymore. Instead, I was back on the bed tied up, but I didn't feel tied up. I still felt like I was sitting on the closed toilet.

Starting to panic, I lifted one of my arms and stared as it moved.

Then, suddenly, I was back in my body.

"Sorry," Nikolai whispered through my thoughts. "It takes me some time to get control of the illusions when I'm tired."

Then I was sitting back on the toilet seat, waiting for whatever signal I was supposed to get telling me that it was safe to make my escape.

It didn't take but a minute before my signal became clear.

In the form of the six-foot-three, muscled man who was my mate.

My very pissed off mate.

The moment he came into the bathroom, I was in his arms, my legs wrapped around his waist, with my hands circled around his neck.

He didn't give us a chance to reconnect, either.

The moment I was firmly in place, he stood back up, and immediately started walking out the door.

Mace waited for us, seeming no worse for wear.

Ian walked in fast strides straight for Mace, practically tossing me on his back as I held on for dear life.

The minute he was situated behind me, we were in the air, Mace pumping his large, hulking wings and taking us far, far away from that shit hole place.

Ian buried his face into my neck while I clutched at his arms.

My fingernails were digging into the skin of his arms, but he didn't seem to care, and I couldn't seem to stop myself from doing it. Now that I was safe again, everything that had happened over the last forty-eight hours began to overwhelm me. It was all too much, and I was on the brink of losing it.

Thoroughly.

We'd been in the sky for less than three minutes when I felt Ian tense behind me, causing me to turn to look at him.

And what I saw over my shoulder had me damn near falling out of the god forsaken sky.

"Shane!" I cried. "What in the ever-loving fuck?!"

"Shane?" Ian echoed. "His name's not Shane. His name is Merrick Brown."

And that's when everything started to fall into place.

CHAPTER 22

I've made it from lying on the bed to sitting up on the side of the bed. There's no stopping me now.
-Ian's secret thoughts

Ian

I was glaring at *Shane*—or Merrick Brown—like he was a bug about to be squished by my boot.

Though, if I had my choice, I would be squishing him. Slowly. With my bare hands.

God, I could gladly rip him apart, piece by piece, until he was nothing but a pile of twitching body parts.

Keifer finally stood, placing a tired looking Blythe down on the chair he'd previously occupied, and pointed at Merrick.

"It's time for you to start explaining," Keifer growled.

Shane looked over at Wink in apology, and then turned back to Keifer.

"My life before y'all was normal. Met Mattie and Wink. We became good friends, and then we lived our lives. Until I turned twenty-one, that was," Merrick sighed. "It started before I was twenty-one, actually. Dogs started showing up randomly at my house. Cats. Fucking birds and squirrels. Then, while I was out in the woods, something happened to me and I was suddenly…more."

"You came into your powers," Nikolai guessed.

Merrick's eyes flicked to the big man who was holding his pregnant mate protectively in the curve of his arms. Once he took in the big man, he nodded, then moved his gaze back to Keifer. "Right. I came into my powers in the woods. About thirty yards away from that cabin."

My brows went up, surprise leeching into me.

That cabin was becoming more and more interesting by the hour.

"Keep going," Keifer said with barely hidden annoyance.

Merrick grimaced.

"My dragon came, but it was at a price."

"What kind of price?" Jean Luc asked this time.

My lips twitched at sight of him.

He was sitting awkwardly next to Mattie, being careful not to touch her. His entire body was stiff and looked uncomfortable as hell.

He was as close as he could get to her without actually touching her.

And it got me to wondering…why was he trying so hard? Was he afraid of what would happen if he did and a bond showed?

But then Merrick's words captured my attention once again.

"My dragon, Sascha, was already owned. The moment our bond came through, though, the previous ownership—or forced compliance on his owner's part—was broken and he was now mine." Merrick looked down. "Sascha hated me. Hated me with a passion, and it took me nearly ten years of trying to win him over before he finally understood the benefits of having me as his dragon rider."

"But…?" Derek, Keifer's advisor and another dragon rider, asked.

"But, what I didn't know, at the time, was that the ownership wasn't completely dissolved. Although Sascha thought it was, it wasn't. Robert had just been buying time until he needed the two of us again." He dropped his head into his hands, looking defeated. "The moment came last year, and that's when I woke up and realized that I didn't have any other choice but do his bidding. He planted something inside of me that forced me to his will."

"The *geis*," I supplied for the others.

Merrick looked at me and nodded his thanks, his eyes skittering past Wink's hot gaze before he could truly read the anger written all over her.

"*The geis*," he confirmed. "I had no choice. Everything that I did was by force, and if I didn't comply, my sister or my friends became targets."

He gave a pointed look at Wink.

"We were never once threatened," Wink shot back. "And since when do you have a sister?"

"He found my sister—who I hadn't seen since we were split up in foster care—and thought she'd do just as well as the others," Merrick frowned. "He tortured her and her mate, but the geis kept me from doing a damn thing about it. And I've spent the last month trying to make everything I fucked up right again. Found my sister's mate's dragon, too. But…," he hesitated. "Can one of you close off this room so what I have to say doesn't leave this room?"

He looked out the window nervously.

Derek waved his hand, and my ears popped.

"Done," he said. "Continue."

Merrick stood up and walked to the window, looking out over the lawn.

All of the dragons were out there.

Every last one of them that was a part of the sanctuary was on the back lawn.

It was definitely a sight to see.

When he got his fill of what he was looking at, he turned to stare at the room as a whole.

"He has more dragons. At least twenty of them."

That statement dropped like a lead balloon in the small room, and the women gasped.

"Fucking shit," Keifer growled. "Goddammit."

Merrick nodded his head.

"And I think…," he hesitated. "I think that one of the dragons is the mated pair to another of your dragons."

My heart started to pound as I remembered the conversation I'd overheard earlier between Mace and Wink.

Wink tensed beside me, and her eyes met mine, fear clouding them.

Wink stood up, but didn't leave my side.

"It's Daya, isn't it?"

Merrick looked up, his eyes connecting with Wink's for the first time since he'd arrived at our sides earlier in the day.

"It is."

"But she died. Mace said so," Wink asked in confusion.

"She is. Almost. She's as close as she can be without actually being dead. A pile of bones and flesh, with no will whatsoever to lift her head or try to eat," Merrick confirmed.

"Then how is she still alive?" Brooklyn asked.

"He's keeping her alive, just like he did me."

Wink's head whipped around, and her eyes bored into mine.

"If he gets her loose…if he finds a way to get her out…can you save her?"

I opened my mouth, and then closed it.

"I don't know," I admitted. "I've only ever worked on a human body before."

Her eyes pleaded with me.

"But you'll try?"

I nodded my head slowly.

"I'll try."

She breathed a sigh of relief and retook her seat.

"What's his agenda?" Blythe asked. "What is he doing? What is he trying to accomplish by enslaving dragons?"

Merrick shook his head.

"I've never been able to figure out why. All I know is what he made me do, and that was help the purists. He's not one…but he's something." He paused, looking torn on what he was about to say. "And I've seen Farrow come into the area five times over the last six weeks."

I stiffened.

Keifer did as well.

"And has he made contact with Robert?" Keifer asked carefully.

Merrick shook his head.

Before I could stop her, Wink shot to her feet.

"He was in your office," she blurted. "He went through your files. Took some and then left when you showed up shortly after he started looking."

I closed my eyes as Keifer turned his angry glare her way.

"He what?"

***

I walked behind Keifer, sure that if I didn't he would likely kill his brother before we got any information out of him.

"Wait, Keifer," I grabbed his shoulder. "You need to calm down. If you go in there all hot and bothered, he's going to clam up before you get anything out of him."

Keifer gave me an evil grin.

"That's why I brought Jean Luc." He pointed at the other man that was walking beside me.

I sighed and picked up the pace, determined to get to Farrow before Keifer.

Despite what he thought, Keifer wouldn't be happy if he didn't get the full story first before he killed him, and I didn't doubt, for one minute, that he wouldn't kill him.

Farrow may be his brother, but Keifer was the king. He had everybody's well-being on his hands. The sacrifice of one, even if it was his brother, was better for his people.

I let him go and raised my hands when he continued to stare at me expectantly. "Just don't come crying to me tomorrow when you feel bad."

His laugh made my stomach hurt.

Yeah, it was doubtful he would ever come to me.

"What's with that look?" Keifer stopped and stared at me.

My brows rose, surprised that he would even notice a change of expression on my face.

"Nothing. Let's go," I grumbled, starting the procession of people forward once again.

Nikolai, Derek, Jean Luc, Keifer and I were all on our way to Farrow.

Farrow lived in his old girlfriend's apartment, and it only just occurred to me how he was living there. Apartments cost money, and Farrow wasn't working. He'd never worked, in fact.

"How did he afford to get this place?" I asked the group as a whole. "I looked over Wink's rental agreement when we first got together." When I backed out of her lease for her and paid the early termination fees. "That apartment goes for upwards of twelve hundred dollars a month. That's a pretty penny for someone who doesn't have a job and hasn't had one in his entire life."

Keifer's cheek clenched.

"I've been wondering much the same thing for a very long time," Keifer grumbled. "And I haven't come up with other answers. I'd hoped by making him responsible for doing the nightly security with you that he'd catch the protector bug, but it only seems to have put him off of doing his dragon rider duties instead of wanting more."

That thought had occurred to me after the one and only night I'd taken him with me on my patrols. He'd been uncaring, uninterested in learning and had decided, early on during that patrol, that this just wasn't for him. Something which he'd said to me multiple times that night.

"He could be selling information on you to pay his rent," I offered.

Keifer's eye started to twitch.

"That would be one of the better case scenarios," Derek mumbled to himself.

Not quietly enough for us not to hear him, though.

The rest of the trip to Farrow's apartment was uneventful, and we arrived at the apartment complex within five minutes. That was the benefit of being a dragon rider, though. We could skim over the freakin' interstates and highways, where traffic was heavy enough that it was backed up for miles, while we enjoyed the freedom of gliding over the road being able to get anywhere without having to stop.

Though guilt had hit me when we'd gone after Farrow instead of Mace's mate.

I knew when Mace finally realized that I knew longer than he, that he wouldn't forget it. Especially if something happened to her while we were working to free her.

I thought it best not to tell him anything until we had a better idea of the situation, and it was more than apparent that Farrow knew more than he was letting on.

Not that he'd told us anything at all.

Which surprised me, because Farrow was usually pretty open about his dislike for all things family and dragon rider related.

We touched down, one after the other, in the back parking lot of the apartment complex, and dismounted.

The moment we were free of their backs, our dragons cloaked themselves and disappeared from view, even though they were all still there.

I could see each and every one of their DNA signatures. Even Farrow's dragon, in the back of the lot, who looked bored and wished he could be anywhere other than where he was.

"Farrow's dragon is here in the back corner of the lot," Nikolai pointed.

"How do you know?" Keifer asked absently.

Nikolai snorted. "Heat signature, brother dear."

Among his other powers, Nikolai could also read heat signatures. If he wanted, he could tell us exactly how many people were in the building we were heading into.

And, apparently, he wanted to, because the next sentence out of his mouth said as much.

"There are twenty people in the complex, all of them but two are on the bottom floor," Nikolai explained.

"Are there two heat signatures in Farrow's apartment?" Keifer questioned as we started to take the stairs.

Derek and Jean Luc took the north set of stairs that would lead to the opposite side of the hallway, and would make sure that Farrow didn't try to make any great escapes.

But, it turns out, the moment we let ourselves into Farrow's apartment, that he wouldn't be making any great escapes. At least not with his woman there, anyway.

A woman who I'd seen dead with my own goddamn eyes.

***

Farrow looked at his brother with his eyes filled with sorrow.

"I needed her. She's my heart," Farrow apologized, looking at his brother like he was ravaged by the decision he had to make.

And I was sure that he was ravaged. Had I been in his position, and seen my own woman get killed, then I would've likely done absolutely anything to change that fact.

"How?" Keifer asked in a deadly quiet tone.

Farrow swallowed, looked over at his girlfriend—cough zombie—and licked his lips.

"It was a…" Farrow cleared his throat.

"Trap," the not-so-dead-woman, Macy, finished for him. "I was killed, and he was sitting there waiting for Farrow the moment he showed."

"He who?" Keifer pushed.

Farrow and Macy looked at each other, and Keifer growled with impatience. "This isn't a time to be contemplating a lie, Farrow. What you'd done has a fucking word, and it's called treason."

"According to Dragon Rider Law, treason is punishable by death. There are no excuses here. Either you are found guilty, or you're not," Derek growled. "And your mate suffers the same fate as you. Now would be a good time to start talking."

I looked over at Nikolai, whose hands had fisted at hearing what Derek had just said, and I wondered if I'd need to pull him off Derek.

Keifer, though, was the one to surprise me.

He looked resigned, like this was what he knew it was coming to all along.

Farrow's face looked ashen, as did Jean Luc's. Jean Luc's parents had been on the receiving end of such a punishment; not by the dragon riders, but by his mom's people.

See, dragon riders weren't the only big, bad entity on the planet.

In fact, there were a lot of fucked up things in this world. Such as the skinwalkers.

Skinwalkers weren't bad, per se, but it was yet to be determined if they were good, either.

Skinwalkers were born to the powers just like we were, but where our power came to us from our dragons, theirs came from sacrifices. Most didn't use sacrifices lightly.

If a sacrifice had to be made, they'd use already dying animals.

In very rare instances, in only of the gravest circumstances, then they'd use healthy animals.

It was absolutely forbidden to use a human sacrifice.

But that's just what Jean Luc's parents had done when they found out that he had cancer. They'd made a human sacrifice, and they'd saved Jean Luc by helping him into not only his dragon rider powers, but also his skin walker powers.

"She's not my mate." Farrow looked over to Macy. "Yet," he added. "Robert bargained, in exchange for bringing her back to life, that I give him information on dragon riders. I gave him some bogus lore, made some stuff up, and mostly told him about my own powers. I didn't tell him a thing about yours."

"What about what we saw you taking from my office?"

"Birth certificate," he muttered, his eyes going to Macy's. "You need a birth certificate to get married."

Keifer's jaw clenched.

"What else?" he pushed.

Farrow shook his head. "I gave him what I had and he's left us alone since."

"And what other powers does Macy have?" Keifer stared at Macy like he was studying a bug under a microscope. "Is she fully alive? What is Robert?"

Farrow swallowed.

"Her heart beats," he was quick to inform us. "But he holds her life in his hand through an artifact."

"Something like this?" I held up the one we'd been able to strip of its power over Wink only hours before.

That'd been Jean Luc's doing.

He'd been able to use his skin walker skills to pull the charm's 'life force' out and put it back into Wink. I'd watched him do the entire ritual and had been amazed while watching him work.

Usually, he was pretty secretive when it came to his skin walker abilities. He saw them as shameful. Something his parents had given him when he'd not wanted them. It wasn't often when he practiced them. Only under very special occasions, he'd informed us.

Lucky for me and Wink that returning her life force to her was a 'special occasion.'

Farrow nodded his head enthusiastically.

Macy, however, stiffened and pushed herself away from it, her face going deathly pale.

"Be careful!" she pleaded.

I blinked in surprise.

"Why?"

"Because they're so sensitive. Anything you do to it, it does to the person who it controls," she licked her lips nervously.

I nodded my head.

"Jean Luc was able to fix Wink right up after we got it from him. When we get yours from Robert, he'll do the same for you," Keifer promised. "But that doesn't let either one of you off the hook."

"How are you going to get it from him?" Macy's voice quivered with unshed tears.

I looked over the blonde woman's features.

She looked much different now than she had the last time I'd seen her, although then she'd had a lovely bullet hole through her heart.

How had I been so wrong about who killed her?

That'd never happened before. I knew exactly who did what based on their DNA signatures.

DNA was a simple thing.

For me, anyway.

I could see exactly who'd been in this room in the last forty-eight hours based on the skin cells that were in the room. If I wished to push further,

I could even go as far as weeks past if I wished to dig that deep.

I, however, didn't.

That took time. Time that I didn't think we had.

"As soon as we find Robert...," Keifer started to say.

"I can help you with that," Farrow told us, standing up. "I can."

Keifer looked at him skeptically.

"And how, exactly, do you plan to do that?" Nikolai piped in.

Farrow stood up.

"I can follow trails. All you have to do is lead me somewhere he's been recently," he nodded his head eagerly.

"I think, after this, you have some explaining to do."

CHAPTER 23

*Mating: when dating goes too far.
-Wink's secret thoughts*

Wink

Brooklyn, Blythe, Skylar, Merrick and I all looked at the newcomer with surprise. We were at the sanctuary, and we'd been having breakfast, when Macy was practically dropped into our laps.

"Take care of her, Skylar," Farrow pleaded. "Can you look her over…make sure that she's okay?"

I licked my lips, my eyes becoming calculating as I wondered exactly why she would need a checkup.

She didn't look sick.

In fact, she looked perfectly healthy.

She must've realized we were wondering why, too, because she smiled and took a seat across from us on the windowsill that overlooked the sanctuary's backyard.

By the time she was finished telling us about her harrowing experience, starting with getting shot, and finishing with being brought back to life by Robert, I was on the edge of my seat.

"That's amazing," Brooklyn breathed. "That's, in fact, beyond amazing. Wow."

I concurred.

The whole thing was fantastical.

"I…," I hesitated when I realized how quiet it'd gotten. "Where did they go?"

"Where did who go?" Blythe looked over at me.

I turned around and scanned the big room.

"It's too quiet," I stood. "Why is it so quiet?"

"What do you mean it's too quiet?" Brooklyn got up to stand next to me. "It's loud. The TV is blaring, and the air conditioner is making quite a bit of noise. Quiet is not something that goes over well when you share a house with fifteen thousand people."

I shook my head and walked to the window.

"Where are the guys?" I asked, starting around the couch to head for the door that led to the back yard.

The house had like fifteen doors that led to the outside, and four of them were on the back wing of the house.

The house itself, was shaped like a E, and we were on the top part of it that housed the great room, the kitchen, the breakfast nook, and a sun room.

The back stretch housed all of the bedrooms, and apparently 'wings' as the others liked to call them.

The entire place was fucking massive, and I found that there was always a buzz of activity.

But today—right now—there was none of that buzz. It was only the TV and the quiet chatter of talking.

"They said to go to the great room where y'all were—which is where Farrow took me, as you can see—and they'd leave once I was safe,"

Macy explained quietly. "Was that bad?"

"They left without us," I murmured, freezing in the doorway. "Skylar…" I started, turning my head to her. "Do you have security footage of the hospital?"

My eyes went to the mini clinic type structure that was housed on the ground floor with an exit to the side grounds, and I studied the area.

"Yes," Skylar stood up. "You'll have to come to my rooms, though. I don't know if I can figure out Nikolai's system off of his."

"I can," Brooklyn said. "But I still don't see the problem."

"There aren't any dragons," I said. "And where are the staff?"

"The dragons are on the back side of the property," Shane—Merrick—said from the other side of the room. "They're having a meeting."

"What kind of meeting?" I turned to my old friend.

Mattie was at his side, and she had her fingers to her lips as she nervously bit away at her fingernails.

"I don't know," he shrugged. "You just asked where they were, and I told you."

"You know where all the animals are?" I asked.

He nodded. "I do."

"What else do you sense?" I pushed.

He looked at me like he wanted to say something more—like an apology—and I shook my head.

Now wasn't the time.

I wasn't sure when that time would come, but right now wasn't going to be it.

Hell, next year might be too soon, too.

He chose to let me have that play, and closed his eyes, concentrating.

I remembered when he used to do this when we were younger.

I'd thought it was just him being a daydreamer. But low and behold, he'd had these abilities for almost as long as we'd been friends and had kept them a secret from Mattie and me all this time.

And I found that it really irritated me.

I would've never broken his confidence had he shared his news with me.

Yet, he'd chosen to keep it to himself, deftly keeping Mattie and I out of that part of his life almost as easily as he'd kept his real identity at bay.

"Forest creatures. Outside the perimeter. Nothing in here," he murmured.

"In here, where?" I interrupted him.

"There's a perimeter that rings the sanctuary about five miles out. It keeps all the baddies away," Brooklyn explained, watching us with worried eyes.

I turned my attention back to Shane—Merrick.

Fuck, I'd never be able to get his name right in my head.

Not when he'd been 'Shane' to me for so long.

"What does it keep out?" I asked just as the room started to shake.

"Not dragons," Skylar said as she walked to the window and looked out. "Not dragons."

I walked with her to the window, and my breath stalled in my lungs.

"Oh, shit."

Dragons of all shapes and colors started to file in over the sanctuary.

One. Two. Ten.

And they weren't any I'd ever seen before.

"Merrick," someone said from behind me. "What's going on?"

I turned to find Merrick behind me, his eyes closed, and his body strung tight like a bow.

"They're not…right."

"What do you mean they're not right?" I asked in alarm.

"He means that they're not right…like me," Macy whispered.

"What…," Blythe started, but her words were quickly cut off by a startled scream that fell from her throat. "My babies."

Then she was running, and we were all running behind her.

CHAPTER 24

Put your laundry away or I'll punch you in the face.
-Note from Wink to Ian

Ian

"They're not here," Farrow said.

I looked around, staring at the empty cages.

They looked old and rickety, and not something that would've held any of our dragons.

What do you think? I asked Mace.

I think that you need to go home, he said easily.

Why?

Because all is not right, he replied.

What's not right? I pushed.

Something.

Shaking my head, I looked over to Keifer. "I need to go."

"Why?" He looked at me incredulously. "You have plenty of time to go do your thing." He pointed to all the things I could go read. "You leave, we have nothing."

I shook my head.

"Mace is telling me to leave. I trust his instincts," I informed him.

Keifer looked at Mace who hadn't gotten any closer than the copse of trees that outlined the edge of the property.

"Fine. We come back after we make sure everything's all right," he commanded.

I nodded my head, and patted the side of Mace's neck. "Home, big guy."

Mace lifted up with a rush of wind, the force of the move pushing me down into his back as he moved faster and faster away from the place we'd just been.

You have more. I told him.

I do not wish to discuss it.

He'd found her DNA. He'd realized that she was there. Was being the operative word.

New DNA looked different from old DNA. Fresher, more vibrant.

I knew he knew with everything I had. But something was keeping him away. Something was telling him to turn back, and I trusted Mace more than I trusted anyone other than Wink. If he said we had to leave, we had to leave. There were no other options.

It was when we were five minutes out from the sanctuary that something in the air changed around us.

Something sinister felt like it was on the horizon, and I knew that whatever it was was going to be bad.

And my fears were realized moments later when one second we were flying through the air as usual, and the next we were plummeting to the ground at an alarming rate of speed.

I, like most other dragon riders, was taught when we initially started riding that the first thing we do in case of an emergency is get to our dragon's feet.

So, I climbed down his neck, and jumped.

He caught me in midair, almost like we'd practiced a million times before, even though we'd never once done it, and he gripped me tightly in his claw.

When we were going through training with Keifer, he'd taught us what his father had taught him. Dragons were large beasts that used their entire bodies to get airborne. However, when a rider was on a dragon's back, they didn't use the full force they were capable of so as not to hurt the rider with the wind shear and drag of their wings rising and falling.

So during an emergency with the rider secured in the dragon's feet, they were able to use all the power of their bodies to gain maximum speed, which was the reason riders were trained to move.

My heart was sprinting at a million miles an hour, and I watched as the ground came at us, faster and faster.

Just when I thought we were going to hit hard, something changed in the air, and suddenly Mace was able to fly once again.

I looked over just in time to see Jean Luc pitch over sideways.

"Catch him!" I bellowed, my stomach dropping when he started to go down in what felt like slow motion.

Keifer was one step ahead of me, reaching out with one long arm and latching onto Jean Luc's unconscious form before he could make it to the ground.

While Keifer was busy catching Jean Luc, Mace was working at pulling us back up, cloaking us both with invisibility that would shield us from everyone else, even the other dragon riders.

My eyes went around to the others, and one by one, each pair of dragons and riders disappeared behind their own cloaks of invisibility.

Keifer was the final visible rider to blink out, and with one last look behind him, he and his dragon were cloaked.

My eyes returned to the horizon, and I swallowed.

"I think we need to drop down," I pointed at Mace. "Just in case that fucker uses those powers again."

I obviously wasn't the only one with that thought, because the moment we touched down on the ground, I heard the others talking.

"It's another skin walker," Jean Luc assured us. "There's nobody else on earth who has those kinds of powers."

I ignored them, continuing the walk to the sanctuary without waiting to see if they followed.

I'd just stepped over the line that denoted the boundary of Dragon Rider territory when I felt it.

Something was not right.

What's going on? I sent my thoughts to Wink.

I don't know, Wink growled. *I just know that something is happening. Something. There are other dragons everywhere, but they're not doing anything but flying around.*

I made my way to the clearing ahead, and froze when I saw the dragons flying over the sanctuary. There were at least two hundred of them.

At least.

"He can't control them," Nikolai murmured at my side. "The way the shield works is that all powers can't be used inside the boundary lines. Well…ours can. But all outsiders can't. I worked everyone's blood into the shield. He might've made it through, but there's literally nothing he can do to us, power wise, besides be in here and do any physical damage he's capable of. Look."

He gestured to the boundary line I could see, and I watched as one of the dragons who'd been unfortunate to re-cross the line was struggling to get back into the boundary.

But the dragon was losing.

That also might have to do with the fact that the dragon was emaciated to the point that she looked like skin and bones. As if she'd not eaten in a very, very long time.

Though that's what all of them looked like in some way, shape, or form.

The silver dragon, the one struggling to get back across, was worse than the rest, though.

I'd just decided to step over to see what I could do when Mace shot out of the cover of the trees, all signs of cloaking gone, and missiled toward the dragon that was struggling.

And it was then that it occurred to me.

That dragon was the other half of his bonded pair, his mate.

Daya.

Mace was only inches away from her when a sudden push had Daya slipping even further over the line.

And that's when I shouted.

"Help her!"

Dragons from all over dropped down from the sky, and I looked over in awe.

But they all weren't moving just to save her.

Some were circling the man attempting to recapture her, preparing to move in for the kill.

The problem was that when they got too close to the line, they started getting sucked in, too.

Smart enough to know that I couldn't go through the throng of dragons, I started running, being careful to hug the edges of the sanctuary boundaries as I went.

The moment I got close enough, Robert, the man from the park who'd tried to take me down, only days prior, was standing there with an intense look of concentration on his face.

And dead human bodies littered all around him.

I watched in horror as he plunged his dagger down into the heart of another human sacrifice, killing her instantly.

Her life blood began to ooze from her and pool around them just as he uttered another word.

A word of power.

"Come!" he bellowed.

I hit him like a ton of bricks, taking him out like a linebacker sacking a quarterback.

One second he was standing, and the next he was on the ground, my fist pounding into his face.

Robert tried to fight back, but the rage I was feeling through my bond with Mace, combined with my own, had me spiraling out of control.

What did snap me back to myself was the knife through my left thigh.

Pain burst through my body as the realization that I wasn't paying enough attention poured through me.

But my reaction time, as well as recovery time, was a whole lot better than most.

That was a plus to being beaten a lot by various foster parents and street thugs when I was a kid into my teenage years.

Before he could think to remove the dagger from my leg, I yanked it out, and thrust it down into his heart like he'd done to the young woman just moments before.

His eyes widened, and his mouth started to part at the edges.

"I'm one of many," Robert coughed. "You may have killed me, but you won't be left alone. Not anymore." Robert's grin was filled with blood as his eyes started to go distant.

I looked at Keifer, who appeared at my side.

Keifer had heard Robert's words.

"Don't." Keifer shook his head.

I froze with my hand on his chest.

"If I heal him, we could get more out of him," I informed him.

Keifer cleared his throat.

"Jean Luc shared his fears with me. I think we know what's going on." Keifer's eyes went to the bodies lying in the grass all around us. "What a fucking mess."

"I think everyone needs to be enlightened to just what in the hell is going on," Derek growled from beside us.

I concurred.

"I agree," I stood up, my leg screaming.

I'm coming

No.

Yes.

I sighed as I saw her start our way, weaving in between dragons who'd collapsed onto the ground in exhaustion the moment they were free of whatever Robert had done to them.

"Let me see," she ordered, snapping her fingers at me the moment she was within a couple of feet.

"What, do you want me to drop my pants in front of everyone?" I drawled.

She turned her glare at me.

"Yes," she snapped. "I do."

Rolling my eyes, I picked up the dagger from Robert's chest, and used it to cut a hole into my pants, ripping the jean material apart until the wound was exposed.

My entire leg had blood dripping down it, and she gasped the moment she saw it.

"Does it hurt?" she cried, dropping down amongst the bodies and the blood.

Before I could protest her doing it, she placed her hand on my leg, and my own power started to stir to match hers.

This was the last place that I would ever wish to have these kind of reactions, amongst the dead and our friends, but my body reacted to hers. And I had no hope against it.

It just was.

My skin started to tingle as the cells started to repair themselves, and within two minutes, pink scar tissue formed over the wound.

"Done," she smiled, happy with herself.

I yanked her up by her arms out of the blood saturated grass, and crushed her body against mine.

The adrenaline was still coursing through my veins, and I couldn't get it to stop.

"I think it would be better if I leave," Jean Luc's rough voice filled the air around us. "It's not going to end. At least, if I'm not here, then we might find a way to circumvent this before it gets out of hand."

No one said a word to disagree with him, and my stomach turned.

I was closest to Jean Luc. He'd been the one and only person to actively try to incorporate me into the daily life of the Dragon Riders.

Without him here, I wouldn't have that any longer.

"No," Keifer said after a while of contemplation. "We're stronger with you. You stay."

A grin found its way to my mouth, and I felt like shit for smiling when tragedy surrounded us.

Luckily, mine wasn't the only smile amongst us.

***

"That's why they kept the dragons for so long," Wink's devastated eyes lifted to mine hours later. "They kept her for her skin. If we'd been only a day longer, they would've skinned her and used her skin to come after us."

We were all clean. Dragons were bedded down in the grass surrounding the sanctuary, their bellies full for the first time in a long time.

The most wonderful thing, however, was seeing Mace and Daya together.

I'd yet to see them for more than five or ten minutes at a time while they were either eating or drinking, but it was enough to ensure that I knew they were both healing.

Daya, when we'd first seen her, had been terribly emaciated. She'd likely been only days away from death, if not hours.

Now, with the heart so close by, and her mate at her side, as well as a belly full of food and drink, she looked like a completely different dragon.

Although, there was no hiding the haunted shadows in her eyes.

Keifer's sharp inhalation had me turning to him, and the grim look in his eyes matched my own.

"It's likely that there are more than just this," I told him. "We need to actively start searching for them."

"And how are we going to do that?" Keifer growled.

"Me," Farrow stepped forward. "I can do this. I already did do this." He pointed at Mace and Daya who were together, their heads touching. "I found them. I can find the others."

"And how, exactly, do you expect me to trust you after today?" Keifer asked. "You've ruined what little faith I had in you."

Farrow swallowed. "What would you do for Blythe?"

Keifer's eyes narrowed.

"Exactly," Farrow snapped. "All this time, and you'd do the same goddamned thing that I did. You know you would."

"You don't know shit," Keifer denied.

"I know that I've been in love with her since I was sixteen years old. I may only be twenty-one and a half, but I know my heart. She's mine. And you continuously took her away from me. I can't begin to count the number of times you dragged me away from her. You tried to tell me to stay away, but I can't. Not with the love that Macy and I have." Farrow stood up straighter. "We…"

"Aren't mated," Keifer snapped. "You have no fucking clue about anything. You've been so far entranced in your own shit that you've never stopped to think about other things. Like, what if you find your mate?" he snapped. "I realize you love her. But your mate, when she comes, won't care that you love another woman. You'll literally kill her and you if you stay away from her. What are you going to do then?"

Farrow's mouth snapped shut.

"I don't do the things I do to keep you from having what you want. I do it because I know what's best. I'm older. I am the king. My word is law."

Farrow bared his teeth.

"I won't accept you separating us," Farrow stood, fists clenched.

"I won't separate you." Keifer said. "Your mate will do that when the time comes." He hesitated. "And when that time comes, when your mate comes, I won't stop you. But until that time comes, you may keep your pet."

Farrow growled.

"That's what she is, is it not?" Keifer challenged Farrow.

"She's going to be my wife."

That dropped like a fucking bomb in the room.

"Farrow," Nikolai stepped in. "Find the dragons. Help us. Keep your nose clean. Stay with your woman. But for yours and her sake, don't marry her. Don't make any hasty decisions, and for God's sake don't think with your cock."

Farrow gritted his teeth to keep the retort from passing through his lips, and I had to give it to him. For once, he was showing that he knew when to shut up.

That was new.

A few hours ago, he'd have given it just as good as he got it, and damned the consequences.

"You have one more chance, Farrow," Keifer held out his hand. "Thank you for helping us today. Thank you for making the right decision. And thank you for saving the dragons."

Farrow looked at Keifer's outstretched hand, and then took it.

"I won't let you down," he promised.

Keifer's smile was sad.

"I sure hope not."

CHAPTER 25

Nothing tastes as good as skinny feels. Except tacos. And cupcakes. Oh, and cookies.
-Wink's secret thoughts

Wink

I made my way out of the spacious room we'd been provided at the sanctuary, and back down the stairs just outside our private suite.

Our new home.

The one that Keifer had demanded we move into.

Though I wasn't the only one that was new to the place.

Jean Luc had been instructed to move in as well…and let's not forget Mattie.

She was situated in another hallway that was meant for single occupants. The single occupants would share a common kitchen and dining area, while the other mated pairs had their own mini apartments to themselves.

I'd just made my way into the large dining room when an amused, darkly erotic voice filled the air.

"A lot has changed since we've been gone," the man drawled. "Can't say that it makes me happy that all the eye candy moves in after we're told to stay gone."

I gasped, turning to face the stranger's voice.

I was wary of strangers, as anyone who'd had a couple of days like I had would be.

And immediately calmed down when Ian wrapped his arm around my neck.

"Mine," he snarled at the man that was sitting on a kitchen chair in front of us. "Mine."

That one was directed a different way, and my eyes widened when I saw the other newcomer.

Both had brown hair and blue eyes, but that was where the similarities ended.

The one who'd addressed me first was introduced as Ford, while the other one that'd been in the corner was introduced as Alaric.

"The last time we were here, no one that wasn't mated was allowed to be here." Ford looked pointedly at Macy and Mattie in the corner.

Then they flicked to Shane, aka Merrick.

"A lot has changed," Keifer said as he came into the room. "Have you been introduced?"

Ford and Alaric both nodded.

"What was the emergency?" Ford asked.

He seemed like a talker, and under different circumstances, I was sure I'd find him a lot more appealing.

However, after yesterday, I didn't find anything appealing but what I knew. And I didn't know these men.

Something I must've made them aware of, because they gave me the distance I needed.

Though that might have been Ian's angry look at my back that was keeping them at bay.

I'd just decided to sit down with a plate of food that Ian had somehow magically produced when something occurred to me.

"There's food moving off the table," I whispered frantically to Ian.

Ian's eyes flicked to the table where a sausage was being pulled off of a plate, and he snapped his fingers.

The sausage paused in its descent to the floor, and I froze when it felt like something had jumped on my leg. Two somethings. One on each thigh.

I was too stunned to acknowledge them. Ian, though, didn't seem too surprised.

"This is Daisy," he grinned.

"*Who* is Daisy?" I asked, my hand itching to sweep down the length of my leg and push off whatever was touching me.

"Daisy," Ian rumbled. "Please?"

Alright, Creepy. What are you doing?

I was about to look at Ian when one of the things on my leg became visible, causing me to gasp.

"Oh, my God!" I cried.

My eyes took in the tiny little dragon on my leg. It was as big as a medium sized kitten in stature. It was solid black with white tipped wings. All except for a small daisy shape on her chest.

"I think you mean, 'Oh, my dragon,' Wink," Mattie murmured, her eyes going wide. "Where in the hell did...," a gasp left her mouth as more and more showed up.

"How cute is she?" I asked, my hand going out cautiously to run one single finger down the tiny dragon's back.

"Cute," Ian rumbled. "I've been trying for six weeks to get her to show herself to you."

My brows rose at that.

"You've kept her a secret for six weeks?" I asked. "How? Why?"

"Daisy isn't allowed to leave the safe zone." He introduced his pet dragon to me. "I think that now that she knows that we're here to stay, she might be a little more accommodating to who sees her."

"Is she bonded to you like Mace is bonded to you?" I asked.

Ian nodded. "Yes, in a way. I named her, and she became mine."

My brows furrowed in confusion.

"They're Fairy Dragons," Brooklyn interrupted. "Fairy Dragons are the smallest of all types of dragons. More like pets than actual dragons. Fierce and loyal. They're indigenous to Scotland and Ireland, and they've never been known to come here before now."

"There are more?" I asked.

Brooklyn nodded. "About 10 in total. Each mated pair has two, one for each person, except for you. Jean Luc, Ian, Derek and Skylar also have one."

"Mmmm," I giggled when Daisy started to chase my finger across the length of my leg.

"Fairy dragons are so rare that they bring out the good in almost everyone," Brooklyn explained. "They're playful like cats and loyal like dogs."

"What's their story?" I asked, giggling when a neon purple dragon appeared to also chase my finger. The other one that'd been on my thigh for the whole time.

This one actually caught my hand, though, and rolled over onto her back as she kicked at me with her back legs like a cat.

"Fairy dragons grow to be about the size of a housecat," Brooklyn explained. "But they're so rare, that no one really knows anything about them. There are a few articles in the dragon archives, but they didn't tell us a whole lot. What I've gathered is that, mostly, they're social creatures who show up when someone worthy is brought forth. Those that can see them are worthy."

"So I wasn't worthy until now?" I guessed, studying Ian's dragon who was glaring at the newcomer dragon like it was an interloper who shouldn't be there.

"You're worthy now because you've got your own dragon, which basically proves your worth," Brooklyn grinned. "I think she showed herself to you out of jealousy because she knew you were about to be taken from her."

"Hmm?" I asked, lifting my hand with a laugh. "My dragon?"

The dragon was clinging to my hand like a monkey, using her wings to wrap around my hand to ensure she didn't fall.

"Your dragon," Ian's head moved, indicating the other dragon that was chewing on my fingernail.

My head tilted.

"I don't understand." I really didn't.

I thought I couldn't have a dragon. I wasn't a dragon rider.

"You don't have to be a dragon rider to have a dragon that's bonded to you," Ford explained.

I looked over at him, met his eyes for only a second, at most, and then couldn't hold them any longer. I let them slip to the side of his face, studying his hair instead of his eyes.

"It's normal," Ian whispered. "His power is to see into one's soul. To know their true thoughts and intentions. It takes a lot out of both him and the person whose soul he's seeing. His dragon has taught him some natural defense mechanisms that automatically repel people from connecting gazes with him."

My brow rose.

"Wow."

"Did you name your dragon?" Ford pushed.

My eyes went back to his face, but this time I looked at his nose.

"No." I shook my head.

Creepy. Something practically shouted at me.

"You didn't say anything in your mind…" he left it hanging, waiting for me to fill in the blank.

"Uhhh," I hesitated. "Can they talk to me in my head?"

All of the occupants in the room, sans Mattie and Macy, who apparently didn't have dragons, nodded their heads.

"Uhhh, then yes, I named her." I started to snicker.

"What'd you name her?" Blythe asked, a sleeping baby against her chest.

"Creepy."

"That's not too bad," Keifer mumbled. "Mine's named 'Little Fucker'."

At that, I lost my battle with my giggles.

CHAPTER 26

Ideas are born from a beard stroke.
-Fact of Life

Ian

I found my wayward mate outside with dragons.

Quite a few of them.

Twenty—big and small—surrounded her while she read from a book.

It'd been two weeks since the day Robert kicked the bucket.

Two weeks of much needed downtime. Although having Ford and Alaric back had a lot to do with that. With them added back into the rotation, I didn't have to go out every night on patrol.

Now, I only went out every fourth night, which was a lot more accommodating for a newly mated dragon rider.

"You gonna come inside any time soon, beauty?" I asked Wink.

Wink, who was resting on the cool grass directly next to Daya, who was still recovering, turned her head in my direction.

"Just let me finish this chapter and then I'll come inside," she grinned.

I knew what that meant.

It likely wouldn't be the end of the particular chapter she was on, but one about two hundred pages later.

Grinning, like the fool I was, I bent down and scooped her up into my arms, causing her to squeak and drop the book on the grass.

"Hey!" she snapped. "That's book abuse!"

I rolled my eyes.

She huffed a sigh of annoyance, and then turned her head so she could look over my shoulder.

"Goodnight, dragons!" she called to the lot of them. "I have to go to bed now, because my mate thinks he knows all. I'll see y'all in the morning! Take care of my book!"

I didn't say anything to her as we made our way through the sanctuary. I nodded at a few of the others who were in some of the common rooms, including my sister, and headed straight for our bedroom.

I didn't stop until I got to the bed, where I gently laid her down and covered her with my body.

"What are you doing?" she gasped.

I hadn't made love to her in over two weeks, since the night she'd told me about her pregnancy with another man's baby.

And that wasn't due to allegations, either, but by her putting me off with bogus complaints of being tired or not 'wanting it.'

I was on edge, and I needed to prove to her that I wasn't upset with her for sleeping with another man before we'd mated.

And I told her so.

"I love you. And this baby," I told her bluntly.

She blinked.

"This baby is wanted. The circumstances that the baby was conceived under weren't ideal, but I'll never take that out against you. Or her."

She blinked away tears.

"How'd you know?" she whispered.

"You've been avoiding it," I mumbled, pushing my hands up the underside of her t-shirt.

Her eyes widened.

"I have not," she lied.

I looked at her.

"Nearly every thought that crosses your mind I'm privy to," I tapped her forehead with one finger. "All except for a select few, and those are the ones that I really want to know."

"What?" she cried. "How?"

I grinned.

"You don't shield your thoughts worth a shit. If I'm in the vicinity of you, then everything you think, I think," I enlightened her. "Everything but the ones that you shield almost automatically. And those I only have to guess about."

"What ones?" she asked stubbornly.

"I get faint hints of what they're about. You feeling bad about mating me when you were pregnant with another man's baby. Not feeling worthy of my love. Things like that." I looked into her eyes. "If I still find you attractive now that you have been soiled."

Her eyes widened in alarm.

"Don't say anything." I placed one finger over her mouth.

She glared.

"But I realized something when Robert died. When I saw his blood on the ground." I started pushing her shirt up and off her body, tossing it across the room and immediately dropping my mouth to place a wet kiss on the soft swell of her belly.

She shivered.

"What?" She asked, quivering slightly.

"That the baby's DNA doesn't match Robert's."

She tilted her head to the side.

"What?"

"The baby's DNA isn't matching up with Robert's." I repeated. "It's matching up with mine."

She gasped and sat up, her face coming only inches from my face.

"What are you talking about?"

I ran my finger across her skin.

"You were right."

She tilted her head in confusion.

"You were right that I was upset that you were carrying another man's baby." I admitted. "Upset enough that I didn't think to look more deeply than the surface. I could see that there was a baby, but the moment I did, I didn't want to be reminded that the baby wasn't mine…so I just stopped looking. Kept myself from seeing that deeply."

She stayed silent.

"And when Robert was lying there, dying, I made a discovery." I told her, trailing my fingertips down the side of her face. "The baby you're carrying is mine."

"How?" She breathed. "You had a vasectomy!"

I shook my head. "I don't freakin' know." I told her. "And honestly, I don't care. I don't care how it happened. Some fucking miracle. Some fucking divine intervention. Whatever it is, that baby inside of you is mine, and all of this shit about you worrying about me loving some baby that isn't mine doesn't even matter anymore."

"I love you," I told her. "All of you."

And then I showed her, making sure to touch my mouth to every single part of her body that I loved.

Her mouth. Her breasts. Her feet. The insides of her thighs.

I left nothing untouched, and by the time I finally got to her pussy with my mouth, she was a quivering mass of excitement about ready to detonate.

I stopped just short of pressing my lips to her clit, and looked up her body.

"You watching?" I asked.

She bit her lip and nodded.

Then I grinned.

"Good."

Then I devoured her pussy, burying my face in her beautiful body and bathing myself in her scent.

By the time I was through with her, I'd wrung out two orgasms from her, and she'd lost the ability to hold her legs up.

"Ready, baby?" I asked her, prowling up between her legs to situate myself snugly against her.

Her eyes were filled with all kinds of things that I liked and, for the first time in weeks, I was able to breathe fully.

That was what she did for me, though. She kept me sane and grounded, which allowed me to just be me.

Notching my throbbing cock with her entrance, I slowly started to push inside, burying myself inside her so fully that there was absolutely no separation between us.

Her lips parted, and her eyes were glazed.

"I love you," she whispered.

I smiled, leaning down to press my lips against hers.

The slight swell of her belly caused my body to bow over hers, and I had a feeling that this was only going to get more interesting as time wore on.

"I love you, too."

We finished together, both of us exploding only moments after our declarations.

"You need to…"

"Don't touch me!" Jean Luc screamed outside our door. "Please, just don't touch me!"

"Jesus," Mattie shouted. "I was just wanting to know if you're okay. Take a breath, and try to, for once, be nice instead of the incredible douche you always are."

"I said don't…"

Wink's eyes widened as a hiss tore from Jean Luc's throat, and what felt like a jolt of electricity poured through our bodies.

"What the hell was that?" Wink whispered to me.

"I think that…" I got up, pulling myself free of her, "was my sister and Jean Luc entering a crazy little thing called a mating dance."

ABOUT THE AUTHOR

Lani Lynn Vale is married to the love of her life that she met in high school. She fell in love with him because he was wearing baseball pants. Ten years later they have three perfectly crazy children and a cat named Demon who likes to wake her up at ungodly times in the night. They live in the greatest state in the world, Texas. She writes contemporary and romantic suspense, and has a love for all things romance. You can find Lani in front of her computer writing away in her fictional characters' world...that is until her husband and kids demand sustenance in the form of food and drink.

Made in the USA
Columbia, SC
19 December 2017